To dear Marjan
Thanks for everything
Nanhee
16/10/03

SAINTLY
SINNER

Typesett in AGaramond

Printed by : Global Printing Services, Delhi (India)
email : globalptgservices@rediffmail.com

Distributed in UK by:
ISHANIKA LTD,
12 Main Avenue
Moor Park
Northwood
Middlesex
HA6 2HJ
T: 08700 270270
E: info@ishanika.com
W: www.ishanika.com

Published by:
Amit Bhatia for
A'N'B Publishers Pvt. Ltd.
O-11b, Lajpat Nagar-II,
New Delhi - 110024
Telefax: +91-11-26929329, 26837725
Email: amitbhatia@anbpublishers.com

NANAK SINGH'S

SAINTLY
SINNER

Translation: Navdeep Suri

This book is dedicated

to my parents

Foreword

$\mathcal{M}$y earliest lucid memories of Nanak Singh, 'The Novelist' to most Punjabis but just 'Bauji' to us go back to my childhood as a six-year old.

The mid-sixties…a sultry night, perhaps in the latter part of June… a large, open courtyard, and a modest three-bedroom house that would expand miraculously each summer to accommodate the extended family as it descended upon Preet Nagar within days of the onset of summer vacations in schools. A row of charpoys arranged in an orderly single file in the courtyard, the family's sleeping quarters for the night but presently functioning as the dining area. A gaggle of kids, maybe a dozen of us, noisily running back and forth to replenish our steel thalis with another chapatti or, occasionally, for a second helping of our all-time favourite – sweet rice, moist and brown from the colour of fresh jaggery in which it was cooked. In the kitchen, Bhabiji – our grandma- squatting on a low stool next to the stove, tirelessly producing hot chapattis for her ravenous army. My mother, accompanied by an assortment of aunts, helped in distributing the food and handling related activities. The kids were fed first, before being shooed away so that the elders could eat in peace.

All the elders, that is, except our grandfather. Bauji was an early riser, often up at four in the morning to pack in a session of writing before anyone else woke up. As a concession, he was often served his thali along with the kids, and the oldest and youngest of the family usually finished eating around the same time. For the kids, this was the time of the day that we would eagerly await. Bauji, preparing to retire for the evening, and the kids flocking around him, tugging at the sleeve of his kurta, and noisily clamouring for one, just one story before he could enter his room. Alright then, you rascals, but just one, he would agree. And so he would be pulled to a charpoy in the courtyard, and we would gather around him. Within minutes, the word would spread…Bauji is going to narrate a story. Soon, the neighbours kids would drop in, and their neighbours kids too. Additional charpoys were brought alongside the one on which he sat. Surrounded by a dozen or so grand children, and often an equal number of youngsters from the neighbourhood, he would start 'Once upon a time…'

And for the next hour or so, as the narrative of an imaginary young hero and his improbable adventures unfolded, he would cast a magical spell over his young audience. With bated breath and unblinking eyes, we followed every twist and turn of the tale. 'Have you ever seen this pack of rascals sit so quietly?' my mother remarked to no one in particular as she came around to clear some dishes. But we were captives, completely spell-bound by the wizardry of the narrative, and unwilling to brook any disturbance by an external element. If the hero landed up in a situation that required music, Bauji would break into a classical raga or a simple ballad to illustrate the narrative. And if he ran into a court jester, the punch line of the jokes, accompanied by the narrator's own full-throated guffaws, would have us clutching our tummies and helplessly rolling with laughter.

Occasionally, he would pause, perhaps to conjure the next scene of the drama, or perhaps simply to provoke the inevitable cries 'What happened next?' Or he would bring the story to a particularly abrupt twist and mischievously suggest 'I think that's enough for tonight! Let us continue this tomorrow!' And wait for the howls of protest 'No, Bauji, No! You have to finish this story tonight! Or we won't let you get up!' He would, of course, acquiesce, and continue to take us through the roller coaster ride of highs and lows before depositing us in a blissful state, ready to go to bed and allow the dreams to take over.

There are other images too, of Bauji dressed as always in a simple white cotton kurta and pyjama combination, returning from his evening walk. A plain white turban on his large forehead, a hint of a smile hidden behind his flowing white beard, a twinkle visible even behind the thick, horn-rimmed glasses that he always wore. Of Bauji dressed in impeccable bandgala coat and achkan, receiving the Sahitya Akedemi's annual award for literature from President Radhakrishnan in 1962; and of me, reportedly cute and chubby, running around in the corridors of Vigyan Bhawan during the ceremony before being picked up by the philosopher-president.

In my mind's kaleidoscope, the time line jumps a few years to 1971 and to the India-Pakistan war that started on 3rd December. Preet Nagar was too close to the border and my grandparents were persuaded to move to our home in Amritsar. Bauji spent much of this time reading, and going out for long walks in the evening. And as the war settled into its own routine of air raid sirens and mandatory blackouts, my friends and I persuaded Bauji to recreate those memorable

Preet Nagar evenings with a new story every night. Within a couple of days, our group had expanded and soon, there were at least seven or eight of us clustered around his bed, hanging on to every word, completely unfazed by the occasional burst of anti aircraft gun fire. It seemed so normal, a bunch of kids sitting around Punjab's greatest storyteller, listening to his tales. Without any inkling that these were going to be his last!

They spent those two weeks with us, until Gen. Niazi's infamous surrender with 93,000 troops to the Indian army on December 17 brought an unexpectedly swift end to hostilities. The following day, they returned to Preet Nagar, and just ten days later, on the 28th, we got a phone call that Bauji had passed away during the early hours that morning. Heart failure, we were told. He left the world as peacefully as he had lived in it, without complaint, and without a moment's bother to anyone. The sense of calm, even fulfilment, was writ large on his face when we saw his deceased body later that day.

Relatives, near and far, started to arrive at Preet Nagar, and as news of the demise of the doyen of Punjabi literature spread, the Punjab government also got into the act. The immediate family's private grief had to be shared with a much larger audience, and even Giani Zail Singh, then Chief Minister of Punjab and later, the country's first Sikh President, made it a point to come for the 'bhog' rituals. For me, barely 12 years old, these events were a blur. The only clear memory that penetrates the haze is of my father and his four brothers at the cremation grounds, and me sobbing inconsolably on an older cousin's shoulder as the funeral pyre is set alight.

Among those present at the funeral was Balraj Sahni, then a celebrated, highly respected actor in Bombay. A couple of years earlier, he had played a pivotal role in the making of Pavitra Paapi into a major Hindi film. A self-confessed admirer of Bauji's writings, he was a frequent visitor and occasionally used our home as a stopover en route to Preet Nagar or on his way back. Elegant, suave and urbane, I remember the stir his visits would invariably create in our neighbourhood. Balraj ji played the memorable role of Panna Lal in the film, and just as we thought we were getting used to his celebrity status, we were playing host to his son Parikshat. Dashing, debonair, handsome to a fault and recently returned after a stint in the West, Parikshat had been chosen to play the lead role of Kedar in Pavitra Paapi. And I do recall at least one matronly neighbour just about swooning when he stepped out of the taxi and walked into our house.

A few months later, I went with my parents to see the film at a theatre in Amritsar. And I remember my absolute amazement over the transformation that the dashing hero had undergone. Because here he was, gaunt, unshaven and dishevelled, living Kedar's life on the big screen. But enough from me, grandson and translator, and over to Nanak Singh- master story-teller- and his Kedar as the Pavitra Paapi, the Saintly Sinner.

Prologue

His Tale, in his Words

*A*las! How I wish I had at least captured an image of his with a camera, if only to offer my readers a clearer image of 'Kamaal'. But little did I know at the time that I might one day be trying to present the story of his life in the form of a 'novel'. And today, I ask myself, will my pen really be able to paint a realistic portrait of that unfortunate soul?

I learnt Kamaal's real name only after he had departed from this world forever, leaving behind only his name. He was generally known as Mr. Kamaal, and for a while, I too took it to be his real name. It was only later that I discovered that Kamaal was more of a nickname, or perhaps a literal way of describing the *miracle* that he truly was. No doubt, whatever I saw of him was nothing short of extraordinary! There was a touch of the marvellous, even of the *miraculous,* in everything he did.

All of this happened quite a while back – about ten years ago, probably around 1931 or '32. But to this day, my feet shuffle to an involuntary halt when I walk past that shop in a busy little street in Amritsar. Although a general merchandise store now occupies the place that used to sell and repair watches, the image etched indelibly in my mind is of a frail youth, probably in his early twenties, wearing a faded brown jacket, crouching in front of a cabinet and repairing a watch with great concentration. The ageing cabinet, its glass exterior cloudy from age and neglect, is the repository of several dozen old watches and small timepieces and numerous minuscule components. A small photograph, maybe about half the size of a postcard, has been glued on the glass panel of the cabinet. From a distance, the photo appears old and somewhat smudged, the features of its object indistinct. A closer inspection, however, reveals that it is a girl of about ten or twelve.

I can still see that watchmaker sitting in the same pose, an eyeglass fitted on his right eye, as he pores over some old watch, prying open its infinitesimal components with a set of pincers and placing them carefully on top of the show case, where they find themselves in the company of several other watches that have already been entirely or partially opened, each in its own little universe within a hemispherical glass globe surrounding it.

I see his thin lips, never without a cigarette between them and always shrouded in a cloud of smoke. And I see the section of wall behind his back, where a patch on the coarse surface has been smoothened out by incessant contact with his scruffy jacket.

Those days, I also had a shop in the same busy little bazaar. His shop, which he started about a year ago, was to my left. Behind his shop was a little room, call it a shed, a dump, or a hovel if you please – that served as his dwelling.

His expertise at repairing watches was legendary, and he could easily fix intricate watches that other watchmakers would be loath to handle. The most antique of models would come to him, as would some of the latest. Whenever other watchmakers failed to unravel the mysteries of a particular watch, they would refer the client to 'Mr. Kamaal'. I know of this from personal experience, because strangers would often land up at my doorstep to ask for directions for Kamaal, the watchmaker!

The word was out in our bazaar that Kamaal must be a seriously flawed character who squandered all of his hard-earned money to indulge some unknown vices. But I always found it hard to accept this view. Why? Because I never saw him go anywhere! From daylight to dusk, he would toil away, and in the evening he would simply retreat into his little dwelling. The only times that I did see him away from his shop was at the post office near the Clock-Tower, perhaps to send a letter or two.

Kamaal was, however, well known for one characteristic: that he could not function unless he had a cup of tea in his belly and a cigarette in his lips. There was, in fact, a remarkable monotony in his life-style. Summer or winter, he would be sitting in the same place and in the same crouching posture, knees almost tucked into the belly, a cigarette between the lips and unwavering concentration in his work. When he got too tired, he would set the cigarette on a cracked china plate and start singing. Always the same song, in the same tone:

Farewell, O fellow travellers of this caravan
Leave me to my fate now
The lonesomeness of a wanderer
Is part of my destiny.

A small, coal-fired stove stood a yard or so away, with a kettle of tea often simmering away on the slow fire. The only time he got up from his work was to pour some more tea, or to use the toilet. He had just one large earthen mug, which he would refill from the kettle every hour or so. And his tea was a strange brew, without any milk and so strong that it was a wonder anyone could drink it at all!

A sagging old bed with a filthy mattress occupied the right-hand corner of his room, while a pile of coal had progressively established its presence on the left. Over the months, the coal had produced a thick layer of soot that now covered the entire floor.

He made sure that his kettle was never empty, replenishing its stock of water from a little pot and dumping a handful of tealeaves into it at regular intervals. Day after day, throughout the year, a trail of steam emanated without pause or respite from the darkened spout.

There was very little about his lifestyle that pleased me, and yet, I found it strangely difficult to dislike him. He had this odd habit of breaking into a loud guffaw every now and then, right in the midst of a conversation. This entirely unnatural eruption would grate on my ears, especially if I was myself dealing with some customers, and would leave me annoyed and irritated for a while. But then he would, equally unexpectedly, start singing those favourite lines of his, and my exasperation would melt away. Not that he sang at the top of his voice; indeed, more often than not he seemed to be humming for his own pleasure. His voice, however, had this strange pathos, a kind of haunting melancholy that would compel me to leave whatever I was doing and start listening to him.

Why was he so frail? This question would repeatedly surface in my mind. Sure, his singing almost had the power to induce a momentary twitch of life even in a corpse. But his gaunt frame was steadily wasting away, his complexion increasingly pallid, as though his flesh and bones were without any blood at all. Yet, his face could not be called unattractive.

I would often catch myself wondering that he must have been quite a handsome fellow when he had the blood of youth flowing through his veins. There were times when even his apparent flaws seemed appealing – his unruly mop of hair, which he would get trimmed once in a blue moon, seemed to be a deliberate ruse to conceal his charm. He had a half broken tooth in his upper jaw, which many would consider a distraction, but to me it only enhanced his attractiveness.

He was a man of few words, but when he spoke, his speech reflected a degree of education and refinement that belied his appearance. Only his guffaws, which frequently punctuated his conversation, struck a jarring note.

His working area was a mess, its cleanliness and upkeep receiving as little attention as his own body. Work appeared to be his only obsession, and he charged a fair bit for the watches he repaired, never accepting less than two or three rupees for a single job. In fact, he developed this rather rude habit of naming his price for a particular job and then refusing to take even a penny less despite the pleading of the customer to negotiate a lower amount. And yet, he had no dearth of customers, often getting more work than he could handle.

I would sometimes try to estimate his income, and my own calculation was that he must earn at least five to ten rupees every day. But what does this idiot do with all that money? I have never seen decent clothes on his body, nor does he seem to spend any money on food other than tea and cheapest kind of cigarettes. Does not seem to have any family, so where does his earning go?? Everything about him was an enigma to me. More than once, I felt like posing him a question or two, if only to see what kind of response would be forthcoming. But without first having a degree of familiarity with the person, it appeared a discourteous thing to do. So I resolved to start spending more time with him.

Some more days went by. I found myself waiting in anticipation for the infrequent moments when I could seize the opportunity to chat with him for some time. Being a Sikh, I had been brought up to abhor cigarettes and tended to intuitively recoil from the smell of cigarette smoke that always engulfed his shop. I also found that exposure to the smoke often gave me a headache. But the desire to satisfy my curiosity would persuade me to set aside these problems and persevere.

He gradually started feeling more comfortable in my presence, and I felt that he also enjoyed our occasional chats. Every now and then, I would delicately attempt to create a setting that would enable me to probe into his cocoon. And each time, my efforts would be met with a broad philosophical comment, or with an equally delicate diversion into another topic.

He was an elusive quarry; every time I felt that I was getting close to him, he would recede a little further away. Not infrequently, he appeared to be the denizen of some distant planet, an alien in these surroundings, unfamiliar with the world around him, and perhaps even with himself.

I was getting increasingly concerned about his frail health. His already spare frame was getting emaciated by the day, his feebleness evident in the manner in which he now needed the support of his hands against his knees to lift himself from his haunches. Each time he traversed the street, I could not help feeling that he would be swept away by the slightest gust of wind. The way he sat on his haunches while working often dragged his baggy pyjamas up to his knees, revealing calves so skeletal that he seemed to be living on borrowed time. To make matters worse, he was working like a man possessed, and poisoning himself with countless cigarettes and innumerable cups of that brew he chose to call tea. And yet, he would guffaw in his usual manner while talking, and his sunken eyes would light up in the same way. Except that the laugh would often provoke a spasm of uncontrolled coughing, ending only with a spit of bloodstained mucus into a dark corner.

I remained relentless in my pursuit, feeling that we were approaching a degree of familiarity that he might finally start opening up to me.

"Mr. Kamaal!" I asked him one day when he had just finished another cup of tea and was coughing in a haze of cigarette smoke, "My friend, why don't you get yourself treated? Your health…"

He interrupted me rather sharply and said, "Treated? What for? Do you think I am sick? You think people who carry a lot of fat around their midriff are healthier? Is being slender a sign of being sick?" And he started to cough as he was speaking. As he leaned forward and spat into the corner, I could not help turning around to note that the mucus was coated with blood. He resumed, "It is wrong, my friend, absolutely wrong. Such comments can mislead, can even demoralize a person. Indeed, to be obese is a much bigger problem than to be slim."

He was responding to a perfectly reasonable comment from me with his own arguments and reasoning, trying to package them with a semblance of logic and philosophy to convince me that he was right. Now, I wasn't exactly naïve and I could clearly see in his eyes that his words were, well, just words. He was not speaking from the heart. 'This man truly is an enigma. An enigma that cannot be unravelled,' I told myself.

A few more days passed, and I could see that his health was now failing even more rapidly. He was still working as hard as ever, but no longer with the same untiring energy.

When I visited him at his home one evening, he asked me, "My friend, would you happen to know an optician? I am thinking of getting an inexpensive pair of glasses. I find that I cannot concentrate on some of the more tiny components; often see double images of the same object."

I was both surprised and angered by his words. Someone who earns as much as eight or ten rupees everyday is seeking a reference to an optician so that he can get a cheap pair of spectacles? I took him to a reputed optician the following day to get his eyes tested, telling Kamaal only that the optician was a friend of mine and would be reasonable in his charges. I did not let him know that the optician was not a friend and that I had secretly paid his full fee so that I could get Kamaal's eyes checked properly.

The doctor's comments after getting the results of his tests came as a shock. "Before I do anything for his eyes, it is important to take him to a good hospital, although I am not quite sure if any hospital would be willing to admit him now," he advised. The doctor gave some eye drops and asked him to come again the following day.

I was searching my mind for some appropriately encouraging comment that would lift Kamaal's spirits. But there was no sign of worry or concern on his face. In fact, before I could say anything, he exclaimed, "That doctor is a fool, a complete ass!" And he guffawed in his characteristic way. "Hospital! Like hell! I am amazed why anyone should go to a hospital at all. As if it is some very desirable place to visit! Life? What is this life…an unmitigated burden, an endless problem! And like fools, we try to cling to it, instead of getting rid of it. It is perverse, this logic. Completely idiotic…!"

I opened my mouth to respond to him but he spoke with such force, such absolute conviction that I found myself unable to summon the necessary courage.

I was now getting increasingly desperate to learn more about him. I was also concerned that if he were to die soon - and there were enough indications of this - the enigma might remain unresolved forever. God knows what secrets were locked away inside him, and I was now becoming quite frantic to know whatever I could.

It was not just his eyesight that was deteriorating; other bodily functions seemed to be headed the same way. He now needed to put his hands around his waist to prop himself up whenever he got up to walk. Sitting at work, he would often start massaging his arms or legs. There was no doubt that his condition was worsening by the day, and I often found myself lying awake at night thinking about him.

And then, finally, just a day before he died, he narrated the entire story that I had been trying in vain to prise out of him.

Winter was at its peak, and the chill winds were like darts piercing the body. It was dusk, and the last rays of the setting sun had faded away. The looming darkness was rapidly swallowing everything that came in its way. I had spent the day frequently distracted by thoughts about the enigmatic watchmaker. Every now and then, I looked in the direction of his locked shop and thought 'Now where the hell has

this idiot gone off? He has never before closed down his
shop in this manner!' I turned away several of his customers
with the excuse that he must have gone for some errand and
that he should be back fairly soon.

I wondered if he might have accompanied that tall, slim,
middle-aged fellow who came to his shop the previous day.
For once, he had set aside his work and I had seen him engaged
in a grave, intense conversation with the stranger, as though
he had met a very close relation after long years.

That evening, as I closed my shop to start walking home,
I passed by his shop and was surprised to note that though
the door was closed, the usual padlock was missing. 'Could
he be inside?' I wondered as my pulse quickened.

I climbed the couple of steps to his door and started to
push it open. With my heart now banging against my chest,
I pushed again, half afraid that I might find myself staring
at a corpse. I called, 'Kamaal, O Mr. Kamaal!' Not receiving
a response, I called again a couple of times and paused. I
thought that I had heard a feeble, barely audible voice. I
was a bit hard of hearing myself, and could not make out
what he was saying. 'A bit louder, please. I didn't get you!' I
called again. On the third attempt, I thought I could decipher
the murmur. 'The bolt,' he was telling me. 'You have to
turn the bolt to open.'

And as I turned the bolt, the door opened and I went in.

What I saw in that darkened room confirmed my worst
fears. He was lying on his charpoy, barely covered as the
blanket had slid over the side. I switched on the light and
found that the room was engulfed with cigarette smoke.
Numerous cigarette butts, matches and matchboxes were
littered all over the floor. The kettle was sitting on the stove

by his bedside, but without any steam emanating from its spout.

He saw me and gave a broad smile that carried no trace of his pain or suffering. But there was a sense of the surreal about the smile. It was a smile, I said to myself, that you would find on the face of a corpse, in the very unlikely event that the corpse decided to smile.

'Mr. Kamaal' I bent over his charpoy and said, 'What happened? I thought you had perhaps left the place for a while."

"Nothing at all! Just felt like resting a bit today. In fact, I was thinking about you. Would you do me a favour and drop this telegram off at the post office?" Saying this, he started to give me the address for the telegram.

"And what would the message be?" I asked.

"Just say that if possible, please come by the first available train." Covering his mouth with both hands, he started coughing.

I virtually ran to the post office, paid express fee and sent off the telegram before hurrying back to his place. He was lying in the same position, his face still covered with his hands.

"Please put a few coals in the stove and some water in…" his words trailed off into another bout of cough, followed by yet another, as he strived to complete his sentence. And when he spat to clear his throat, a shiver went down my spine. Instead of mucus, it was blood, just blood.

Paying heed to his words, I stoked up a fire in the stove and picked up the kettle. It was nearly half full with old tealeaves. I emptied the kettle, washed it and filled it with water before putting it back on the stove. As the water came to a boil, I picked up the tin containing tealeaves and put some into the kettle. He pulled himself up and grabbing the tin from my hand, emptied the remaining tealeaves into the kettle. "That much?" I asked. "This would be enough for twenty persons!"

"I have to do the work of twenty five, not just twenty persons, Mister. Today, in particular, I should have added even more tea but unfortunately, this is all I had."

I looked at him in wonder. He had one foot in the grave, and yet he was talking as though he actually believed that he had the strength to do the work of twenty persons.

"And why should you be adding extra tealeaves today?" I asked him as I walked across to open the little window at the back of the room. I was feeling suffocated by the clouds of cigarette smoke and the fumes now coming from the freshly added coals.

"Because today, there is a lot that I must talk with you," he said as he turned on his side.

"And to talk, you need the tea…?"

"Tea and cigarettes – those are the only two things that I live on," he said even before I had finished my sentence.

"So go ahead! Start!" I said, barely able to contain my anxiety to finally learn more about this enigma.

"Can a motor run if you don't provide it with petrol and lubricants?" he smiled and asked me. "Though I will not counsel you to drink the tea, because you will find it tough to digest more than a couple of sips."

"How many cups do you drink in a day?" I asked.

"Never felt the need to count," he smiled back.

"And cigarettes?"

"I do not even try to keep track of those."

"Idiot! You should have at least *some* concern for your health!"

"But it is precisely *concern* for my health that makes me do all this. You think tossing around on this bed all night would be better for me? This way at least, I have a cup of tea and can sleep for half an hour or so. And when I wake up, I make myself another cup. So I am taking care of myself, aren't I?"

His words were filling me with anger and revulsion. 'What a miserable existence?' I thought. "What do you propose to do when you run out of money, and find that you are no longer capable of working? What would you do then?" I asked him with an edge in my voice.

By now, he had already polished off three cups of tea. Setting the kettle back on the stove and lighting a cigarette, he said "You are perhaps wondering if I have saved something for my funeral? Let me assure that it would not be an unreasonable concern on your part. As a good neighbour, you should be worried about such matters. But what you do not know is that I have been dead for a long time. An old corpse does not need much of a funeral, although if you feel like it, you could certainly muster something. As for me, I am neither worried about it nor particularly care for these things." He yawned as he finished his sentence and said, "Would you please pass me the kettle again, and the cup too?"

Sipping the tea again, he said, "So you think I drink this stuff because I like it? No, Mister. No. For me, this tea serves the purpose of water for fighting a fire. This hot water that I drink may not be able to smother the fires smouldering inside me but at least it keeps them from exploding into flames. Because if they do get out of control, they would burn me into ashes in no time at all. Ah! So you smile? But there is no reason to smile, my friend. I know that I would have been finished a long time ago if I had not resorted to these methods. I sing, and laugh, and put up an act all the time. Do you know why? To fool myself – and to forget what I am. You, and several others, have often advised me that I should go to a doctor, get myself treated. Do you fellows really think that any medicine or treatment is going to make a difference to my condition? No! Because that is impossible! But for the sake of make believe, let us assume for a moment that there is this miracle doctor who has a miracle drug that can actually cure me. This begs the question that why should I do something so stupid as taking this medicine, when I know that death is the only, and indeed, the preferred solution for me. You know the proverb 'Only the wearer knows where the shoe pinches'. Well, when you are in my condition, you don't ask the doctor for a medicine to cure you. You ask for an injection so swift and effective that it would take away your last breath even before it has penetrated your arm."

The stench of cigarettes, the pathetic condition of his house and his own ghastly appearance – I was oblivious to all these. Swept off my feet by the flow of his words, I found myself willing him to carry on. And he did, alternating between the tea and cigarettes, his lips seldom free of one or the other. He was perhaps consuming both with a much greater fervour today, finishing off the entire kettle and asking me to replenish it with water again, insisting that the tea in the kettle still had enough strength for a few more rounds. Reacting crossly to my hesitant attempt to inquire about his health and to check how he was feeling, he said, "Please don't waste my time in foolish talk. There is a lot more that I must tell you. You don't have to worry about my health. Haven't I already told you my views on this?" With this reprimand, he started narrating the story of his life, seemingly drawing fresh energy from every kettle of tea and every emptied pack of cigarettes. His voice gave no hint that this was a man speaking from his deathbed. And he spoke continuously, pausing only when his frame would be wracked by another bout of cough and another expulsion of bloodstained mucus, or when he found himself out of breath.

His tongue had started to falter, and to lapse into the occasional stammer. He tended to lose the train of thought every now and then, at times mixing up the sequence of events or repeating himself or pausing to remember what he had been talking about. But he kept talking, for maybe an hour and a half or more. And his pace quickened just as his narrative appeared to be concluding.

Towards the end of his narrative, it seemed that his strength was deserting him, that he was virtually pushing himself to somehow get the words out. Fearful, I tried more than once to stop him from speaking. But he would disregard any attempt, any interruption, and continue, somehow or the other. And he spoke on, and on, and on.

When he finally finished speaking, I noticed that his eyes were shut. I have to confess that what he said was enough to move the toughest of souls, let alone one like me who is essentially a poet at heart. And for a while, his words mesmerised me to the point of actually diverting my attention from his rapidly waning condition. Jolted back into reality when he finished, I saw his head slumped on his shoulder, as though without the energy to lift it. The kettle and the last pack of cigarettes were almost empty.

I nudged him and called his name a couple of times to wake him up. After a brief silence, he responded in a worried tone "It is quite late now. I think you should go home."

I told him that I would be happy to spend that night at his place but my words merely provoked the angry retort "Why? First, I have no intention of dying so soon, and even if I have to die, I would like to be left absolutely alone."

I did not want to leave him that night, but when I realized that my presence there was clearly making him uncomfortable, I reluctantly dragged myself away. Before leaving, I asked him one last time "Mr. Kamaal, if you allow me, I could fetch a doctor to see you."

"Upon my oath, you will not do so," he crackled as he turned his back to me and called, "Do switch off the light as you go."

I switched off the light and turned the bolt to close the door behind me. Heart overflowing with emotion, I trudged back home. For some reason, I felt a strong urge to cry out aloud. I wanted to go to a place where none could hear me crying, none could see my tears. The tumultuous hour and a half that I had spent listening to his story had created a deep turmoil inside me.

Around midnight, unable to sleep and increasingly restless, I got up once again. His face simply refused to go away as I tossed and turned, cursing myself, 'What have I done? Was he in any condition to be left alone?' I put on my clothes, picked up the lantern and was about to leave when my wife called, "Where are you going in the middle of the night, in such severe cold?" I replied that our neighbour, the watchmaker, was unwell and that I was just going to check on him.

Once again, I turned the bolt, opened his door and switched on the light. As I glanced at his bed, the lantern almost dropped out of my hand. Kamaal's head was tilted to one side, his body was stiff, and there appeared no sign of life.

I approached him and felt his arm, which was hanging over the side of the bed, just above the overturned kettle. There was no need to feel the pulse; his arm was cold and stiff. An empty cigarette pack lay by his side, and the fire in the stove was almost out, the last few coals reduced to a heap of embers.

I heaved a deep sigh and went out to call some of his immediate neighbours.

The following day, before carrying out his last rites, some of us went through his meagre belongings. Most of the neighbours expected to find at least two or three thousand rupees stashed away in his house and were shocked when they did not find a single penny. His words 'Everything I have will finish together' were resonating in my ears. Besides, I believed his story that he actually had no material possessions.

The tragic manner in which he died, and the words in which he narrated his story, left a profound impression on me.

I knew that the Bombay Mail from Rawalpindi arrived at 12.30 in the afternoon. Having sent that telegram the previous evening, I was fairly certain that some relative or friend of his would surely come by that train and I delayed his funeral procession accordingly.

It was around one o'clock that afternoon when a tired looking horse pulled a *tonga* to a halt near the crowd. A couple disembarked from the *tonga*, made their way through the throng and embraced his body. The man was the one I had seen at his shop a couple of days back. And the heart-rending sobs of the woman would have brought tears to the eyes of the hardiest of souls. The time of cremation was approaching and the two still had their arms around the body, seemingly unable to let it go. It took substantial effort by several of us to eventually pull them away so that the funeral procession could begin.

Today, ten years after the demise of that unfortunate soul, I remember him once again. And it has taken a strange coincidence to bring those memories back.

On 28 July 1942, I came to Lahore from Preet Nagar. Unable to finish my errands during the course of the day, I decided to spend the night with a friend in Lahore.

The windows of the first floor living room of my friend's house overlooked the busy street below. Exhausted from the day's exertions, I pulled up the arm chair before the window and sat down to gaze at the bustle of cars, rickshaws and tongas passing through the street.

My eyes suddenly settled on the building in front. Across the street from my window, I could see the shop of a Muslim watchmaker. Light bulb dangling above his head, the watchmaker was crouching over a cabinet, repairing a watch. He was sitting on his haunches, in a pose that instantly reminded me of my interlude with that unfortunate fellow almost a decade ago and once again, his image started floating before my eyes.

Memories of the story that he had narrated started such a vivid train of thought that the entire episode started swirling around in my mind, taking the form of a novel.

I asked my friend for some plain paper, and started giving shape to the story that I had heard almost ten years ago. The story of the Saintly Sinner, of "Pavitra Paapi".

Preet Nagar
Nanak Singh
15.10.42

CHAPTER 1

"What happened? Is everything okay?" Maya looked at her husband's crestfallen face and inquired.

"Nothing," Panna Lal replied, averting her querying gaze as he entered the house. But Maya could see that this *nothing* was definitely concealing something. Depositing young Inder Kumar in Veena's arms, she followed her husband into the room.

Their family, living in a modest little house near the top of the street, was passing through a great deal of stress as they tried to cope with the vicissitudes of life. Panna Lal felt like a bird that was only moments ago flying high in the blue skies but now, hit by the errant pellet of a shotgun, lay fluttering on the ground. As the owner of a flourishing business, he had seen prosperous days. But unexpected losses in his trade had abruptly reduced him to a situation of extreme penury. From a position of employing clerks and accountants at a monthly wage of fifty or sixty rupees, he found himself working at a shop for just thirty-five rupees a month. Wealth, as they say, is truly a transient shadow, vanishing as suddenly as it appears. The owner of substantial houses and properties was now having to manage in a humble dwelling – a dwelling which had escaped the tidal wave of financial losses and debts that had obliterated everything else of value only because in some prescient moment, Panna Lal had registered it in his wife's name. Not that he had any dishonest intent in doing so; just the concern that if all else were lost, the family would at least have a roof over their heads.

Troubles, of course, have this uncanny knack of coming in relentless waves. One after another after another, Panna Lal had taken so many blows in recent times that they had sapped him of strength and vitality. His once healthy frame had lost considerable weight, and his endless worries seemed to be draining every ounce of blood from his body.

The sun was setting and it was a pleasant evening in the early days of spring. But the husband and wife pair formed a picture of absolute despair as they sat facing each other.

How could the wife remain unaffected when her husband was in this state? Deep down, perhaps, she was even more dismayed; but there was one big difference between Maya and her husband. Though a woman, she possessed a masculine spirit and did not allow sorrow or anxiety to overcome her. Whenever she saw Panna Lal slipping into despondency, she would try to lift his sagging spirits with the simple words, 'If those days did not remain with us, these too will not last long.'

Maya is about thirty years old, maybe about five or seven years younger than her husband. But at first glance, he appears twice her age. Though not quite as healthy as she once was, Maya's frame does not show any visible signs of the turbulent times that her family is facing. There is a certain freshness in her complexion and she has not allowed financial hardship to diminish her good looks. Despite bearing four children, she looks a lot better than many women of her age. Her elder daughter Veena is now fifteen, and Vidya, the younger one is twelve, followed by the two sons.

If Panna Lal's difficulties were limited to managing his household within his meagre income, he might not have been quite as desperate. Households can be run with more money, or with less. One way or the other, things could be managed within his wage of thirty-five rupees. But there were two major problems that were slowly sucking his blood like leeches. The first was his business losses, which not only wiped out a wealth of twenty or twenty five thousand rupees but also left him with some outstanding loans. The saving grace was that after settling his accounts, he could escape going to jail and thus retain some self-respect in society. He had kept the issue of unpaid loans a secret from Maya, thinking that she may not be able to take this double blow. Meanwhile, the burden of interest on the loans was mounting by the day.

The other problem, even more serious than the first, was the responsibility of arranging the marriage of the two daughters. In Veena's case, the matter was more pressing. They had already accepted a proposal from a good family and with the wedding date approaching rapidly, Panna Lal's worries too were growing exponentially.

Entering the room, Maya saw her husband reclining on the bed, his pensive countenance providing unspoken evidence of his burdens. Sitting by his side on the bed, she put her hand on his arm to pull him towards her and asked, "What's wrong? You are…" Maya saw the tears streaming down her husband's face and sensed that some major calamity had occurred, or, perhaps, was imminent. It felt like the quiet before a storm as Maya fell silent and braced herself for the impact of the words that she would soon be hearing.

Panna Lal finally broke the silence without waiting for her to repeat her query. Inhaling till his chest could take no more, he let out a deep sigh and said, "I just cannot understand! Why is fate playing such cruel games with us?"

"Pray tell me what has happened," Maya steeled herself and whispered gently.

"They've sent a letter." Panna Lal reached into his pocket and started going over the text on the postcard he was holding.

"Who has sent it?" Maya inquired, apprehensive that she might already have guessed the identity of the sender.

"Veena's in-laws."

"I *knew* this was going to happen," Maya spoke with rising anger. "I could feel this coming. I've been having bad dreams since several days. So, what have they written? That they want to go back on the engagement?"

Panna Lal nodded to signal 'yes' without uttering a word.

"To hell with them then," Maya declared. But behind the bluster, her heart was writhing in agony. She wanted her feet to take her to some place far away where she would never have to hear such words, nor feel the pain over the fate that had befallen her unfortunate daughter. She rose, as though ready to do something, then sat down again and said, "Don't worry. If one door has been closed, a hundred others will open. Our daughter will get married wherever her destiny lies. Daughters aren't going to remain at their parents' homes forever."

"But for us, all doors are now closed," Panna Lal heaved another deep sigh and said. "The gateway to death is the only one that remains open…"

"Stop voicing such dark thoughts," Maya interrupted him. "It's all a question of fate. There is no dearth of boys and if we don't get a wealthy family, we'll get a poor one." But her heart shuddered as she thought, 'My gifted daughter, whose beauty can light up the darkest corner! Will I now have to foist some beggar on her?'

"Anyway, would you please read out what they have written?" Maya asked her husband, thinking that she might perhaps be able to clutch at some straw in this dismal situation. But Panna Lal neither said anything nor made any effort to read out the letter. He simply did not possess the strength to do anything that might scratch his already raw wounds. Maya's eyes moved away from his face and were now transfixed on the post card that was trembling in his fingers.

"Mother! Please tell Basant to behave; he is being really bad. Keeps dipping his fingers into the inkpot and rubbing them on my face," Veena said as she entered the room, carrying the toddler in her arms. Veena's slender face showed an ink stain that she had clearly tried to rub off. In the process, she had managed to create a bigger smudge that looked a bit like the map of Ceylon on her cheek and made her innocent face appear even more attractive.

Veena had large blue eyes that enhanced her beauty manifold. She was passing through that delicate stage between childhood and youth. A mere glance at her back tended to quicken the pulse and increase the desire to see her face. Her jet-black hair was braided into a long, serpentine plait that twirled around her slim, fair neck to create a magical effect. Her attire was simple, yet appealing. Her knee-length, waist-hugging *kameez* was complemented by a parrot green *salwar* that revealed glistening white feet, not unlike the crescent moon as it peeps from behind the clouds. When she spoke, her voice sounded like the gentle strumming of the strings of a sitar playing in the fifth note. Her hands were lovely too, with slender fingers capped by lilac-coloured nails. And when she opened her mouth, a cool breeze emanated from the even, pearly rows. At times, when she was in a thoughtful or pensive mood, her long eyelashes would come down to cover her shining eyes. Occasionally, she would lisp slightly while uttering the letter 'a' but even this was done in a way that the listener would wait eagerly for her to lisp again. A little beauty spot on the side of her nose drew the admirer's attention to her face.

Veena was in the 9th grade in her school, while her younger sister was in the 6th. Veena was not unaware of the desperate situation in her home, and the worried look on the faces of her mother and father often saddened her deeply.

She had entered the room to complain about her little brother but a wave of shock ran through her when she saw their expressions and observed that they stopped talking as soon as she walked in. Seeing the post card in her father's hand, she instantly sensed that something was seriously amiss. Forgetting about her own complaint, she approached him and asked, "What is that letter about, Bhapaji?"

Maya gazed lovingly at her and said, "It does not concern you! Please go outside and play with the child. I'll come soon and teach that Basant a lesson."

'*It does not concern you!*' Veena withdrew from the room thinking about it, feeling that somehow the issue that her mother said 'did not concern her,' must indeed concern her directly. She wanted to ask her mother again about the letter but the customary timidity of a young girl in such matters discouraged her from pursuing the issue openly. 'I must find a way of reading that letter,' she said to herself. And her desire to discover the contents of the letter was stoked further when she saw her mother close the door behind her. Veena was now convinced that the letter had everything to do with her and surmised that it must be from her future in-laws.

She deliberately walked out through the courtyard without stopping where Vidya and Basant were playing. Basant thought that Veena had gone out because she was still angry with him.

A charpoy stood upright beneath the small rosewood tree outside their main door. The neighbours' cow stood nearby, along with a calf tied a few feet away to an old wooden plank. The calf was straining at the rope to reach its mother's udders but was frustrated in its endeavours by the insufficient length of the rope.

Veena pulled down the charpoy into a horizontal position and sat the toddler on it. To keep the child busy, she tugged at a low branch from the tree and broke a small stem that he could play with. The letter must be from my in-laws, she thought as she too sat on the charpoy and recalled the words of her friend Channo. Channo was from Gujarkhan, her in-laws' town. It was, in fact, Channo's mother who had brought forth the proposal for the marriage. Veena's in-laws and Channo's parents lived a short distance from each other, and were also somehow related. So Channo not only knew Veena's fiancé but was also a distant cousin of his.

Whenever Veena and Channo met, the issue of the forthcoming marriage would dominate their conversation. Channo would sometimes tease her by calling her *bhabi* or sister-in-law, an expression that was guaranteed to provoke Veena's ire. But Channo could see that the anger was largely a put-on, and a sense of barely concealed pleasure lay just beneath the surface. Having succeeded in needling Veena, Channo would try to create an opportunity for them to chat privately. They would retire into some quiet corner of the house, or take the stairs to the rooftop terrace in the evenings and whisper away for hours. And Channo would narrate highly embellished accounts of Veena's fiancé, her descriptions frequently going well beyond her own knowledge of him. She would often go something like this…he is very handsome….he has his own bicycle….he sings really well….he is a great story-teller....his family is quite wealthy....they have two houses, three or four wells, five or six shops...whenever I go to Gujarkhan, he asks me about you....they also have an orchard....he often thinks about you....and so on.

Veena sat in a reverie, repeating Channo's phrases in her head. An imaginary portrait, painted by Channo's colourful images, swirled around her. 'If the letter is really from them, what could they have written that has upset my parents so much', she wondered. 'Maybe they are pressing for an early marriage? But that would be something to celebrate! How can anything related to marriage ever be upsetting?'

In Veena's world, *marriage* was synonymous with joy and happiness. Marriage could *not* have any other meaning. Every single marriage that she had ever seen had been nothing but celebration – a pageant of singing, dancing, music, fire-works, wonderful gifts and dowry, banquets and parties, and much, much more.

'So that letter must be from someone else,' Veena reflected, putting her train of thought on an altogether different track. 'But if it is from someone else, why did they attempt to hide it from me? Whatever the case, when Bhapaji comes home in the evening and hangs his jacket on the coat-peg in his room, I will try to sneak in and read it,' she decided.

Veena remained lost in her thoughts for a long time, her trance broken only when she heard her mother's shout, "Veena! I thought you were looking after the child! And here he is, stuffing those leaves into his mouth! He could choke on them!" Maya grabbed little Inder from the charpoy and put a couple of fingers into his mouth to prise out a leaf before stomping off into the house with him.

CHAPTER 2

Sardar Attar Singh's shop was situated in Raja Bazaar in Rawalpindi. He sold watches, running the biggest wholesale and retail establishment in 'Pindi. He was the sole agent for West End Watch and several other reputed companies.

Like other gods and goddesses, Lakshmi, the Goddess of Wealth also tends to favour those who are most devout in their fervour. Attar Singh was certainly one of the most ardent devotees of this particular Goddess. The wealthier he became, the sharper was his desire to see his wealth grow even more. Parting with any cash at all pained him as though the money was literally cutting open his heart to escape. In his entire life, he had seen just two places – his shop during the day and his home at night. He had never been spotted at any *gurudwara*, or at any community gathering, or even at a public function. He had not one but two reasons for this. First, his preoccupation with his business did not give him any time to do anything else, and second, his body had attained such a bulk that simply going from home to office and back was a very considerable project. In earlier days, he used to live some distance from the shop and getting to work was a real problem. Walking, of course, was quite impossible, and his size would discourage any tonga from accepting his custom. Occasionally, an avaricious tonga owner would agree to take him, but only on the condition that he would have to pay for the exclusive use of the tonga and not have the option of sharing the fare with other passengers. The exclusive tonga fare could come to as much as eight annas, a price that was not merely excessive but well-nigh unbearable for a soul with Attar Singh's disposition. Parting with eight annas for going and the same for the return journey meant a full rupee down the drain daily – thirty rupees in a month, and three hundred and sixty five over the course of the year!

He managed, eventually, to come up with a solution for this predicament. He moved his family to an attic above his shop. The inconvenience of going down the stairs and then climbing them again once a day would often get him annoyed, especially since the stairs were much too narrow for someone of his size and he tended to scrape and even bruise his shoulders during the journey. But there was no alternative, he reasoned. One must learn to manage, one way or the other.

His acquaintances would often advise Attar Singh: 'Sardarji, the Gurus have showered their blessings upon you. Why don't you spend five or ten thousand rupees and make yourself a nice house.' To which Attar Singh would invariably laugh and respond "I am not an idiot that I should blow up such vast sums of money on a foolish project. Do you know what the interest on ten thousand rupees would be? A hundred rupees a month! Twelve hundred rupees in a year! Imagine where that figure would reach in ten or twenty years! In these difficult times when money is so hard to come by, spending so much on a house is nothing but stupidity."

Panna Lal was employed at Attar Singh's shop. Strictly speaking, his job was to keep accounts. In practice, however, he had to do all sorts of chores, from being an all-purpose clerk to buying groceries for the household to whatever else he was asked to do. Panna Lal had now worked there for almost five years. He used to get forty rupees a month, but last summer the owner had cited a recession in the market to reduce his salary by five rupees. This did not mean that Attar Singh was not concerned about his employee. Otherwise, he would not have continually pestered him to acquire the watchmaker's craft. It was Panna Lal's misfortune that he could not profit from the advice. Despite more than one effort at learning the trade, Panna Lal's poor eyesight had proved an insurmountable obstacle.

Panna Lal's inability to follow his advice would frequently irk Attar Singh. 'If he can get thirty five rupees every month without lifting a finger, why should he bother himself with those tiny components,' Attar Singh would mutter to himself. Although Panna Lal had often tried to explain his helplessness, Attar Singh was not convinced. 'Mere excuses,' he reasoned. 'Paying such a large some of money every month for keeping accounts alone is beyond my capacity.'

Attar Singh had sound reasons for urging him to learn the watchmaker's craft. He was confident that if Panna Lal could repair some watches, he would make enough to pay for his salary and maybe even yield a surplus. He believed that his shop could attract a fair amount of business for repairing watches. But to hire a watchmaker just for this – and pay him at least fifty rupees a month? Attar Singh did not consider it a viable proposition. If only he could get a person who could be an accountant and also a watchmaker, he thought wistfully.

When Attar Singh realized that there was no hope of making a watchmaker of Panna Lal, he started to look for ways to find the right person for his requirements. But his discreet inquiries had not yielded any results so far. The burden of paying thirty-five rupees every month for an accountant felt heavier by the day but he also recognized that he was quite dependent upon Panna Lal. His own education was

rather limited and he needed someone who could handle
the accounts and also manage the correspondence with various
commercial organizations. And so Attar Singh agonized over
his dilemma. He could not fire Panna Lal until he got an
adequate replacement. And he could not help feeling that
Panna Lal was getting his salary for free!

CHAPTER 3

$\mathcal{P}$anna Lal could not sleep a wink that night. His life had become darker and more frightening than the night itself. Every sentence of that letter seemed to be casting its own shadow of death upon him. He could feel his heart sinking. As he lay tossing and turning, he kept repeating the same lines in his head –'our son is not ready for the marriage yet. If you are in a hurry, you can arrange some other match for your girl…' He thought 'If the boy is not yet ready for marriage, it would be a minor matter. It is not as if our daughter has become too old. We could easily wait for a year or two. But why did they write 'if you are in a hurry'…. It is a clear hint that they are reluctant to go ahead with the marriage. Is that because I am no longer their equal? Would they have written such a letter if I still had my earlier status? What will I do now? When people learn that my daughter's engagement has been broken, I will be unable to go anywhere, nor face anyone in our community. And the burden of unpaid loans keeps increasing by the day. God forbid if Maya ever finds out that we owe almost two and a half or three thousand rupees! How will she be able to take it? Moreover, the other girl will also be ready to be married of in a couple of years. How are things going to work out? How will this floundering boat ever find its shore?'

Panna Lal woke up fairly late that morning, with the feeling that he did not have the strength to get himself out of bed. His world seemed an ocean of darkness – dark when he closed his eyes, darker still when he opened them. The

walls appeared to be closing in on him, ready to devour
him at any moment. For a moment, he thought 'Why don't
I just forget about everything and go somewhere far away?
Wouldn't that remove the root cause of the entire problem?'
But then the image of his four innocent children and their
mother would come before his eyes and he would curse
himself, thinking 'Is that why I brought those kids into
this world? Is that why Maya's parents married her to me?
No! No! It would be a sin, an act of cruelty, even treachery.
But what else can I do? ....What...?'

Veena walked into the room, running a largish comb
through her long tresses. "Bhapaji, aren't you going to get
up today? Sun's been up for a long time," she said.

Panna Lal looked wistfully at that beautiful creation of
Mother Nature and thought, 'It would have been so much
better if I did not awaken till doomsday.' Rising slowly
from his bed, he went upstairs to the roof.

Thinking about the letter, Veena looked around like an
anxious doe before dipping her pale, trembling hand into
her father's jacket. Sneaking a couple of quick glances at
the door, she took the letter out and breathlessly went over
the text. The colour drained out of her cheeks as she read
it, her glistening eyes blurring momentarily before she checked
herself. Returning the letter to the pocket, she quietly left
the room.

Panna Lal had washed up and was getting ready to go to
work when Maya stopped him to inquire, "So what have
you decided?"

Panna Lal opened his mouth to reply but no words
emerged. It was a question for which he did not have an
answer.

Her husband's silence sent a nervous shiver down Maya's spine. Though she had been worried since the previous night, Panna Lal's bewildered, speechless look had the effect of a heavy rock that virtually crushed Maya's spirit under its weight. Knowing fully well that neither Panna Lal nor anyone else on the face of this planet could provide her an answer, she repeated her question and said, " No use letting your spirits droop like this. We have to come up with some solution." Her words carried a hint of determination, as though she had arrived at some decision.

"What can I say…?" Panna Lal could utter no more than this.

"I suggest," Maya started gently, "Sell off the little jewellery that I have. It should fetch us at least three or four hundred rupees, and you could approach the Sardar to loan you another three or four hundred. We will try to manage somehow within twenty rupees a month, and the remaining fifteen can be deducted from your salary to settle the loan over a period of time. If we can arrange this amount, we might be able to persuade those wretched fellows. I am sure there is just one thorn pricking them – whether we can provide a decent dowry in our present state."

These words were spoken by the same Maya who had said the previous night, "There is no shortage of boys. If one door, is closed, a hundred others will open…." But right now, she was trying to do whatever she could to appease the same in-laws.

Panna Lal saw merit in Maya's suggestion and felt that he could perhaps discern a faint glimmer of hope in his wretched existence. "But if they still don't agree?" he asked.

"Why won't they agree?" Maya spoke with great assurance. "I will go and persuade them. Now, please go and try your best."

"And if the Sardar turns down my request?" Panna Lal said with a sinking heart.

"Would you at least go and try!" Maya said angrily. "Why must you be such a pessimist about everything? Why should he turn you down? Five years you have worked for him. Never once have we asked for a penny. Even a mere acquaintance can be expected to help you in your hour of need. And daughters, in any case, are a community's shared responsibility. Why the reluctance? Just go and cajole him a bit to plead your case. And if you can't persuade him, I will go to the *Sardarni* and ask for her help."

Her words gave Panna Lal some strength and encouragement. He found a touch of life returning into his steps.

As he walked towards the shop, he found himself alternately sinking or swimming through turbulent currents. At times, he would think, 'I am sure the Sardar will agree to help me when I explain my situation to him. After all, he too has children of his own; he will feel my pain.' But then, his mind would take a different turn and he would argue, 'That miser! He who hates to part with even a penny! Who finds it a burden to pay me thirty-five rupees after getting me to work non-stop for ten hours every day! How will he give me several hundred rupees?"

And so, his spirits at times sagging and at times lifting, Panna Lal approached the shop. His heart was thumping against his chest. With each step his heart would echo like the rhythm of feet dancing to the beat of a *tabla*, 'If he says no…. If…?

He finally reached the shop. Sardar Attar Singh was reclining against his large, round cushion. A little distance from him, near the cabinet, was a frail young man, sitting on his haunches, his knees resting near his chest. He had clean, sharply defined features and would have been in his early twenties. His clothes were soiled and in tatters, and his appearance showed signs of complete neglect.

Panna Lal had to reply to some pending letters that he had been unable to finish the previous day because the Sardarni had called from upstairs that their son seemed to be coming down with measles. Panna Lal had left his work where it was and taken the child to a doctor. Entering the shop, Panna Lal said 'Sat Sri Akal' to the Sardar and was heading straight for his table at the rear of the room so that he could get the pending letters out in the first post of the day when he heard the Sardar call, "Panna Lal! Please come this way for a minute."

He asked Panna Lal to sit down and asked him, "How much salary do I owe you till today? Could you please work it out and let me know?"

Panna Lal was stunned by this extraordinary question. Before he could open his mouth to ask what the Sardar meant, Attar Singh said, "Hadn't I told you several times to learn a bit of the watchmaker's craft? Why would I have to engage someone else if you had done so? This fellow has a B.A. degree and can also repair watches. Now, you be the judge and decide – a B.A. pass versus a 10th grade fail? And then, the watchmaker's skills for free! Do you know what salary we have agreed upon? Twenty-five rupees! I am sure you will not feel bad! After all, there is nothing personal about this. It is all about running a business! If you were to get a job today that offered you fifty rupees, it would be selfish on my part to insist that you should be stuck at my place for thirty five rupees, wouldn't it?"

The Sardar pointed towards the young man and said, "Hand over charge to him and also calculate your remaining salary. If I remember correctly, you had drawn some advance last month."

Panna Lal's pupils froze, as if they had suddenly lost their sight and movement. He felt that the shop's ceiling had unexpectedly collapsed on his head. He turned his head to look first at the stranger, and then at his boss. His tongue had thickened and throat dried to a point that he could not utter a word. He started to get up, then sat down again, his head still reeling under the shock of the blow.

The young man was looking searchingly at Panna Lal's reaction. He finally pulled up a chair next to Panna Lal to look at the books. Panna Lal felt the words on the accounts ledger expand all over the page. He saw lines merge with each other, and then grow until they would fly off the page. The more quickly he wanted to leave the desk, the longer it was taking him to finish the task. He was afraid that his heart might not stop beating while he was still at the desk. He rubbed his eyes repeatedly to clear the dense fog that was clouding them but the words still appeared dim and distant. As he explained the accounts to the new clerk, he made mistakes at several places and most of the figures had to be corrected two or three times before they finally tallied.

After handing over the accounts, Panna Lal calculated his salary. Settling the advance that he had drawn left him with a total of twenty-six rupees, which he half-heartedly thrust into his pocket as he nodded goodbye to his boss and started retracing his steps without having spoken a single syllable during the entire process. As he neared his home, he felt like some mysterious force was weighing his feet down, stopping him in his tracks.

He stood rooted to the same spot for a long time before finally turning around and taking the road that would lead him out of the city.

CHAPTER 4

When Kedar entered the real world after finishing fourteen years of education, he found himself alone in this vast, unknown sea of humanity. There was none that he could call his own. His father had been a man of modest means, a watchmaker who toiled hard and saved whatever he could to give his son a decent education. Kedar had not yet passed his F.A. when the cruel hand of Death snatched his father's comforting shade from his head. His mother dipped into the family's meagre capital to ensure that he could somehow complete his B.A. To see her son get a B.A. degree was her greatest desire. But she was not to have the good fortune to see his graduation certificate. She unexpectedly fell ill and went into a deep sleep from which she was never to rise again.

Kedar was a hard-working and dedicated youth from his early days. He also had remarkable perseverance, and would not give up until he had finished his task, no matter how small or large it might be. He was also exceedingly sensitive, to the point that any kind of emotional disturbance had an inordinate impact on him.

He was twenty-one or twenty two at that time. Although it is quite normal for most persons to be attached to their parents, in Kedar's case, the affection was so great that he felt he could not live without them. The trauma of his father's death was still fresh in his mind when he found himself deprived of his mother's love and support too.

From the time he started his education, Kedar had this dream that he would study hard and get a degree so that he could make enough money to provide a life of comfort and luxury for his parents. His sole ambition was that his parents should be able to live like kings and he should enjoy the pleasure of serving them. But in an inaudible voice and a language that he could not comprehend, the Goddess of Fate was saying, 'Kedar! Why do you build such lofty castles? Your dreams are soon going to turn into unfulfilled aspirations.'

It was like a bolt from the blue when God snatched his mother from him. Kedar felt that there was nothing left for him in this world. He cried and wailed, and for several weeks, he locked himself up in his house and brought himself to the point of starvation. But would this bring him back his lost paradise?

His mother used to tell him, 'Kedar! When you pass your B.A., we will get you married. A beautiful bride will come....' And like a child, Kedar would bury his head in his mother's bosom and say, 'Mother! Don't you dare say such a thing! Would you want someone else to steal the love that I hold for you? I would never let such a thing happen. I would even spurn God's own affection if there were a chance that it would take me away from your love.'

The same modest little home that was his paradise when his mother was around would now torment him as soon as he set foot inside the house. His friends and neighbours tried their best to comfort him. 'Kedar! Your parents can't always be around. Each one of us has to depart from this earth when He calls. Now, you have to be strong so that you can stand on your own feet.' But Kedar paid little heed to the advice. For him, these words were like water off a duck's back.

After several days in this twilight zone, Kedar had an abrupt change of heart. Without telling anyone and without a destination in mind, he left his home. A mere twenty rupees was all he had in the house and this was the amount that he set off with.

Without any aim or purpose in mind, Kedar wandered from place to place. He would start walking in the morning, and would sleep at night wherever he had reached. When hunger became overpowering, he would get a couple of *chapattis* from any roadside eatery and quench the fire inside his stomach.

He found rather suddenly one day that his limited financial resources had been completely exhausted and he was confronted with the stark question, 'What do I do now?' This fundamental query quickly made a very large impression on his psychological condition. He was not far from Rawalpindi, the biggest city in the vicinity. 'I will find some job in 'Pindi.' The thought quickened his steps, and driven by his hunger, his pace progressively increased.

By the time he reached 'Pindi, his empty stomach made him feel like he had mice gnawing at his innards. Impatiently, he started his search for employment and found quickly enough that there were no jobs sitting around, waiting for him to turn up. Throughout the day, he trudged from one shop to another but without success. After many days on the road, he wore a haggard look that led most persons to quickly conclude that he was either a beggar or a vagrant of some sort. His insistence that he held a B.A. degree also had the opposite impact. People now thought that he was a lunatic and taunted him.

He passed that night hungry, lying at Mai Veeron's embankment, a place frequented by a number of beggars and mendicants who had nowhere else to spend the night. Gazing at the stars that night, he recalled that he had also learnt the watchmaker's craft from his father. Why not try his luck at some of the shops that sell watches!

He got up at dawn and set off to find these, stopping finally before a fairly large shop that retailed watches in Raja Bazaar. The shop's Sikh proprietor sat in a semi-reclining position against a large pillow and appeared to be counting something with his fingers. Seeing one who looked like a beggar before his shop so early in the morning, he admonished, "Move on! Move on! Stop blocking the entrance. The day has hardly started and these beggars are here already!"

"Sardarji, I am not a beggar," Kedar gently protested.

"So, what are you?" the proprietor asked sharply.

Kedar opened his mouth to say that he had a B.A. degree but stopped. He had already paid the price for this folly. "Sir! I can repair watches," he said.

"Repair watches? You?" Examining him from head to toe, Attar Singh said, "Liar! Is this what a watchmaker looks like? What a charlatan! Get lost!"

Kedar spoke with great humility, "Excuse me, Sardarji! The world looks at a man's external appearance and starts estimating his intelligence and knowledge. I can do a lot, but right now I am nothing…just an unfortunate stranger who hasn't had a meal for a long time but who would prefer to die than to beg money so that he can eat. I have not come to seek alms, only to ask for a chance to do honest labour. If you give me a watch to repair, I will at least be able to earn a meal."

Listening to him, Attar Singh thought, 'Such a cultured voice! Such a refined dialect! Such articulation! Can these belong to a beggar or a vagrant?" He asked Kedar to sit on the platform at the entrance of the shop and, tossing him an old watch, an eyeglass and a screwdriver, said, "Let us see if you can open it and put it back again."

Kedar finished the work in less than twenty minutes, leaving the astounding proprietor to inquire, "So, can you read and write a bit?"

"Yes, Sir! I have a B.A. degree."

"A B.A. degree?" the owner chortled in mirth.

"You could test me in that too," Kedar said as he looked hopefully at the proprietor.

"Here! Read this," the proprietor fished out an envelope that had come in the morning's mail from beneath his cushion and handed it to him. Kedar opened the envelope and took out a letter that was typed in English. He quickly read it out and then translated it into Punjabi for the proprietor's benefit.

A wave of elation ran through Sardar Attar Singh's flabby, unattractive face. 'This fellow could be extremely useful. If only he is dependable with cash.' He rained a barrage of questions at him, and found that he was receiving a satisfactory response to every one of his queries. Feigning a complete lack of interest, he finally said, " I don't really need anyone right now but seeing your pitiable condition, I'll try to help you. If I employ you as a watchmaker and clerk, how much salary do you want?"

"Sardarji, I only need enough for food and clothing. I will accept whatever you can give me. I am a single man and do not have any family to look after."

"Fine! I'll pay you twenty five rupees a month, provided that you work with dedication and honesty."

"Thank you. I would have been satisfied with a lesser amount too. I will not say anything about my dedication and honesty right now. Let time alone be my testimonial."

"Why don't you come inside and sit properly," Attar Singh said. He was annoyed with himself. 'I have acted in undue haste. He would have gladly accepted twenty instead of twenty-five. But I have now committed, and it is not proper for a man to go back on his word.'

He turned to Kedar and said, "My employee will be coming soon. He will explain all the paper work to you. And let me have a list of the items you need for the watchmaker's job."

"I'll do that, Sir. But if I could have some money first, I will quickly go and eat something. My empty stomach is driving me crazy."

"Sure. Take as much as you want," Attar Singh said as he put his hand into his pocket. Seeing Panna Lal approach the shop, he withdrew his hand and said, "My clerk is just coming in. Why don't you spend a few minutes to learn about our accounts from him? After that, you can take the rest of the day off. You can eat properly and also get some soap and wash your clothes. Wearing dirty clothes to work does not create a good impression."

"As you say, Sir," Kedar said even though he was worried that the pangs of hunger would not allow him to concentrate on anything.

He proceeded to take charge from the old employee, and we have already read what happened during this process.

Panna Lal left after handing over charge and collecting his salary. But Kedar's hunger had suddenly vanished. The expression on Panna Lal's face, and the words uttered by the proprietor had made everything crystal-clear. It is said that a forlorn soul can always spot a compatriot, and has a genuine respect for his sorrow. Kedar was already repenting that he had robbed a needy man of his livelihood. While Panna Lal was handing over charge to him, Kedar thought more than once that he should remove himself from Panna Lal's path but somehow found himself unable to do so.

As Panna Lal left the shop, he gave Kedar a look of such anguish that it seemed to pierce straight through his heart. He felt that with that one look, Panna Lal had thrown a very heavy curse upon him. Satisfaction at having found a job deserted Kedar completely, leaving him with a feeling of remorse so strong that its flames threatened to consume him.

CHAPTER 5

$\mathcal{I}$t did not take Kedar too long to have a meal, get a haircut and wash his clothes. He finished all this in three hours or so and returned to the shop to quietly resume his work. When the proprietor looked around to glance at him, he could scarcely recognise that it was the same person who had arrived that morning. Attar Singh took out a few old pocket watches, a timepiece and an ancient clock, along with the watchmaker's tool-kit. He needed a watchmaker more than he needed a clerk.

Attar Singh was in the habit of sleeping for an hour or two during the afternoon, and as he turned around for his siesta, Kedar started to open the watches so that he could clean and repair them.

He had completed repair of two of the watches and was going to start on the third one when a middle-aged Muslim man came in, handed him an envelope and said, "Mr. Panna Lal asked me to deliver this letter to you."

"To me?" Kedar inquired incredulously. "Who is Panna Lal? I don't know anyone in this city."

"The one who used to work in this place," the man said as he departed. Kedar opened the envelope and as he read the letter, a tremor ran through his hands. He stood up and looked around in fear, as though he wanted to run somewhere – to catch someone. Sitting down again, he started reading the letter one more time, perhaps to reassure himself that what he had just read was, perhaps, merely a delusion. The letter said:

"My saviour! You did well by coming to rescue me from my wretched existence. Most of my optimism had already been swept away by the rising currents of despondence. There was just one ray of hope left, albeit a faint one. And it was with this expectation that I had come to the shop today. You have done a great favour by not just crushing that last hope but also snatching from me the means of feeding my four children. Now, all prospects have been finished. There is no other objective for which I should stay alive. Everything I had is gone and I have not the slightest hesitation in accepting death. In fact, I am now heading towards its embrace, so that I can be rid of all my troubles and sorrows.

"How will my four children and their unfortunate mother fare after me? I am continuously haunted by this fear. Yet, this fear can no longer restrain my steps because I realise that even by staying alive, there is precious little that I can do to get them out of the web of misfortunes that has ensnared us. So I am now headed for the place from where there is no return.

"I don't quite know why I am addressing this letter to you when I know that you are not only a complete stranger to me but are also the cause of my death and the misery that is going to befall my children. Perhaps I have written these lines because I wanted you to know that, thanks to you, I am bidding eternal farewell to my job and to my life. I want to die at a place where there is none that knows me, so that my wife and children are spared the shock of my death.

"I would like to congratulate you for getting your new employment, but would add that by taking this job you have committed a sin so grave that you will not be able to atone for it even if you are reborn seven times. You will never be able to get happiness and your soul will never be at peace. This is my curse upon you.

Panna Lal"

After reading the letter a second time, Kedar tried to read it yet again but found himself unable to. He could hear lines from the last paragraph echoing inside his head: 'you have committed a sin so grave… you will never be able to get happiness… your soul will never be at peace…'

He stood up. The proprietor was awake by now. "I'll be back soon," he said and left the shop in a hurry without even waiting for his consent.

He still had 11 annas from the rupee the proprietor had given him in the morning. He hired a tonga and rushed towards the railway station.

Paying 10 annas to the tonga owner, he bought an entry ticket with the remaining one anna and hurried inside. He searched every nook and corner of the station, scanned every train but found no trace of the person he was looking for. Dejected, he finally left the station and aimlessly wandered the streets till late in the afternoon before returning to the shop with a heavy heart. The proprietor was impatiently waiting for him. After Kedar's abrupt departure, he had checked the two watches he had given for repair. Attar Singh had been overjoyed to see that the near useless watches were now as good as new and in perfect working condition. He told himself that at this rate, this fellow could be like the proverbial goose that lays golden eggs. But with the delay in Kedar's return, he was beginning to get quite anxious. He was worried that he should not meet the fate of the one who remains on the horns of a dilemma and can attain neither God nor Wealth. His former employee was gone, and he feared that the new one might have vanished too. He heaved a big sigh of relief as he saw Kedar return. He was angry at the manner in which Kedar had absented himself on his very first day of work but did not consider it wise to vent his anger at such a valuable person.

Kedar mumbled some excuse about getting delayed in returning to the shop and went back to his work. But his mind was in a state of utter turmoil.

By nightfall, Kedar had repaired one more timepiece and also finished the accounts for the day. Attar Singh now had to grapple with another problem – accommodation for Kedar. He said, "Kedar, it's too late tonight to do anything but tomorrow, I'll try to find you a room somewhere. I suggest that you could sleep tonight on the platform outside the shop. I'll send you a charpoy and bedding from my place upstairs." Giving him five rupees for his dinner and other requirements, Attar Singh locked the doors from inside and took the stairs at the rear of the shop to his home.

As Kedar lay down on the bed, his mind was in a state of severe disquiet. Every little while, he would suddenly spring up, as though he had just been stabbed in the side. He felt like his body was trapped in a cage and the bars were closing in on him. Feeling neither hunger nor sleep, he sought to hide himself from his own eyes. Time and again, those three phrases would come like an earthquake's tremor and shake his very core. 'You have committed a sin so grave... you will never be able to get happiness... your soul will never be at peace...'

Kedar gazed at the people still in the bazaar as they passed by the shop and thought that they must be going to the court to file a petition against him. He was afraid of everything that surrounded him. Every passing tonga or car gave him the feeling that they were crushing Panna Lal's body under their wheels as they went by. He looked at a Kashmiri labourer as he trudged past with a heavy burden of firewood on his back. The wood must surely be for the funeral pyre of someone who has just died, he told himself.

His attention turned towards a tall, good-looking young woman walking hand-in-hand with a boy of seven or eight. They must be siblings, he thought as he saw them come towards the shop. From some distance, she first looked at him as he lay on the bed outside the locked doors of the shop and then peered at the signboard above the shop's entrance. Kedar's eyes followed her as she bent to whisper something into the boy's ear before deciding to walk past. They went past another couple of shops down the street before stopping and turning back towards him. Kedar could see the girl nudging the boy to go towards him but the boy would resist and try to push the girl to go instead. In this pushing and nudging, both ended up going back the way they had come.

Kedar's eyes kept seeing their images long after they had left. He found himself intrigued by the girl's beauty and was still thinking about her when he saw them coming back towards him. This time, they came fairly close to the shop before they stopped. The girl took a few hesitant steps towards him, and the boy also followed her. She was now virtually next to his bed but had not yet uttered a word. She glanced at him and seeing an obvious query in her glistening eyes, Kedar could not help asking her, "What's the matter, Bibi?"

"Do you know about my Bhapaji?" the girl asked him warily and with a degree of apprehension.

"Your father?" Kedar sat up and asked. "What's your father's name, Bibi?"

"Panna Lal," the boy standing behind her said before she could respond. "Our Bhapaji has not come home yet."

Kedar did not have to pose any further question. The girl said, "My Beyji has not eaten anything since morning. She is very worried."

Kedar found himself paralysed. He searched for a response but could say nothing. He returned to his senses when the girl repeated, "Maybe you don't know! He works at this shop."

"I know," he managed to say as he checked the surging tide within him with great difficulty.

"You know?" the girl's eyes lit up as she posed the query. "Where is he?"

"He had to leave by this evening's train for Bombay, Bibi." Kedar said, unable to come up with a better story.

"Bombay? Bombay??" the siblings queried in unison.

"Yes, Bombay. Sardarji wanted an old transaction with a company in Bombay sorted out and decided to send your father for this."

"But…but why didn't he inform his home before leaving?" The combination of fear and surprise made the girl's innocent eyes appear even more attractive.

Kedar felt a pain surging so strongly within him that he was sure it would soon burst its banks and come flowing through his eyes. All the lies he was telling the girl seemed to get caught in his throat, unwilling to emerge until he virtually prised them out. "The train…the train…time was very short," he heard himself say as he turned his face to quickly wipe his tears. "Before he left, he told me to inform your home but I didn't know where exactly you live," he managed to complete his sentence.

"We live in Bhatara Street near Chaudhry Bhola Nath's house," the girl said softly.

"Fine. I'll come there in the morning and explain everything to your mother.

"Why don't you come right now? Beyji won't eat anything," the girl said, her eyes now moist.

Kedar reflected on this for a while before responding, "If I come now, I am afraid that someone might steal my bedding. I will positively come tomorrow morning. You tell your Beyji that there is nothing to worry. She should have her dinner."

The girl's expression indicated that she was not quite convinced. "If you would come with me now, I could leave Basant here to look after the bedding," she hesitantly suggested.

Kedar found himself facing an awkward dilemma. He pondered on the issue some more and said, "Well! If it were unavoidable, I could have come right away. But…but I will come tomorrow morning. Definitely. Now you be a good girl and go home."

The girl lifted her head to repeat her demand again but restrained herself. In the light of Kedar's response, it would seem impudent. She was turning around to go home when Kedar asked, "What's the name of the street again, Bibi?"

"Bhatara Street."

"Bhatara Street? Fine. I will be there in the morning. You go home and take it easy now. By the way, what's your name, Bibi?"

"My name is Veena," the girl said as she clasped her brother's hand and left.

The way she said that last word 'Veena' sounded like the melodious note of the musical instrument after which she was named, and had much the same effect on Kedar's ears.

CHAPTER 6

There are times when you get a premonition, in one shape or form, of a catastrophe that is imminent. When Panna Lal left home for work that morning, Maya stood in the doorway and gazed at his back until it had receded far into the distance. For a fleeting moment, she wanted to run after her husband and call him back. But why, she thought as she held herself back. As the day went by, Maya's disquiet increased. Although her life these days was seldom without anxiety of one kind or another, today was different. She felt strangely restless and uneasy. On normal days, Panna Lal would leave for his work and she would take bath and change before busying herself with the day's chores. But today, she could not bring herself to do any of this. She assigned some of the household tasks to Veena and went into her room to lie down. Here too, she was relentlessly assaulted by all manner of negative thoughts that only reinforced her fears that something was amiss.

It was lunchtime and Veena had managed to put a meal together in the kitchen. Maya wanted that as usual, she should feed the kids properly but feeling that she would be unable to drag herself out of bed, she asked Veena to take over this responsibility as well. Maya was in the habit of having her food only after she had made sure that Panna Lal had eaten properly. He normally came home between noon and one in the afternoon but it was past two today and Maya's concern was growing rapidly. Every few minutes, she would go to the door and peer down the street to make out if she could

see him coming home. Or she would ask Basant or Vidya
to do likewise, only to be told each time that 'Bhapaji hasn't
come yet.'

An hour passed, and then another. It was now four o'clock
and Maya had not eaten anything. She waited, still expecting
her husband to walk in at any moment. There had been
times when excessive work had kept Panna Lal tied to the
shop and he had only come for lunch around four. Indeed,
she even remembered occasions when he had not come home
at all during the day - when he had taken his lunch from the
bazaar and had only returned after closing the shop in the
evening. Maya reasoned that something similar must have
happened today as well. Only a few days back he had
mentioned that he literally had to do the work of two persons
these days. But she had never felt the kind of unease that
she was experiencing today.

It was dusk, and then night fell. Dinnertime had also
passed and there was still no sign of Panna Lal. To Maya,
each passing moment felt like an eternity. Finally, unable to
wait any longer, she asked Veena to take Basant along and
inquire at the shop. When they returned empty-handed after
a considerable time, Maya's heart sank. Though she felt
somewhat more stable when Veena told her about her father's
sudden departure for Bombay, her anxiety was now turning
into bewilderment.

"Who gave you all this information?" Maya asked,
knowing that her husband was the only employee at Attar
Singh's shop. Although he did have a couple of commission
agents who would procure orders for his products, they lived
in their own homes and not at the shop.

"Veena! Who was he?" she asked once again.

"Some stranger."

"What did he look like?"

"Slim, with a fair complexion. Quite thin, actually!"

Maya did not ask any more questions. She spent a very uncomfortable night, waiting impatiently for the morning. Veena had told her that the stranger would himself come in the morning to provide further details about Panna Lal's abrupt departure for Bombay.

Maya rose earlier than usual that morning and busied herself with tidying up the house. She took bath and washed and dried her hair, dressing up perhaps because the stranger was to visit them.

It was around 7.30 when someone called 'Veena!' from the street. Maya was lying on her bed, while Veena was mopping the kitchen floor. Hearing her name being called, Veena quickly tucked the mop into a corner, washed her hands and ran to open the door. She returned soon with Kedar. Maya had also heard him call and was already waiting in the doorway. Seeing Veena bareheaded and in just a shirt and petticoat, she directed sternly, "Go inside and complete your work!"

As Veena went into the kitchen, Maya lowered the *dupatta* over her head and replied to his greeting of 'Namaste' with folded hands. Taking him inside, she offered him a chair and herself sat on the floor at a respectable distance.

"No, Bibiji. Please don't sit on the floor," Kedar said as he got up from the chair. His courtesy and thoughtfulness immediately made a positive impression on Maya, who got up and sat on the bed near the chair.

Veena, in the meanwhile, quickly finished cleaning the kitchen and changed her clothes before re-entering the room to sit beside her mother.

Kedar knew that he would be bombarded with a flurry of questions as soon as he arrived and had also worked out the answers that he was going to provide. So he himself broached the subject, saying, "I told Veena last night that her Bhapaji had to leave for Bombay somewhat unexpectedly. As you know, Bibiji, an employee is an employee, even if he works for a king. The way he left without even informing anyone at his home is, of course, quite extraordinary. But then, he was also in no position to decline his employer's instructions. I arrived from Bombay yesterday. A dispute with a company there over some agency agreement had to be resolved. Accounts that have been outstanding for several years also had to be settled. The matter became urgent because a firm from Lahore is also trying to obtain representation for the same company. Sardarji wanted to make sure that he does not lose the company's business and so he decided to send your husband to Bombay immediately."

The positive first impression made by Kedar had already allayed some of Maya's fears. His good looks, gentle demeanour, measured tone and soothing words gave Maya the sense that half her sorrows had been shared. She said, "*Bharaji*, I wouldn't normally worry about this. Carrying out the wishes of the employer is a matter of religious duty for us. But I was more concerned about the fact that he went empty-handed, without any change of clothes, any bedding...."

Kedar interrupted her to say, "He has everything he needs. I had extra bedding, and also some spare clothes in my suitcase. I forcibly loaded the suitcase and bedding on the tonga as he was leaving. He is an unusually saintly soul. Kept insisting that what is the need for all these things. Now, you tell me Bibiji, how can anyone manage in a strange place without clothes or a bedding?"

Kedar's words were like balm on Maya's wounds. Her heart showered blessings on the kindness of this stranger.

"Bharaji, you have really put yourself to a lot of inconvenience," Maya said with a feeling of deference for the young man. "How will you manage after giving him your clothes?"

"No, Bibiji. I will not face the slightest inconvenience."

"But how long do you think he will have to stay in Bombay?"

"It could take a week or so."

"And when did you come here?"

"I arrived yesterday. I'll be managing his work at the shop until Mr. Panna Lal returns."

"But why did you sleep on the platform outside the shop?"

"I haven't been able to arrange any accommodation yet. Maybe I'll find a place in a day or two."

"You should have come home, instead of sleeping out on the platform like some stranger."

"No problem, Bibiji. I was quite comfortable."

"And roughly how much do you propose to spend on renting a place?"

"About four or five rupees a month."

"Ah! For that amount, you could rent a place next door that has been lying vacant. They want five rupees but I am sure they will agree to give it for four."

"If you could please take the trouble of arranging it for me?"

"No trouble at all, Bharaji. I will check up today. The landlady is a very decent soul. Why don't you go and take a look to see if the place appeals to you?"

"I am sure I'll like it," Kedar said as he opened his wallet to give his solitary five rupee bill to Maya and said, "Please take this and give them a month's rent in advance."

"There is no need to pay an advance, Bharaji. Please keep the money," Maya said and returned the money. Kedar took it and put it back in his wallet.

"I would still prefer that you took one look at the place," Maya said and looked at Veena. "Why don't you go with him, Veena? Take the key from Aunt Indu and show him the house."

Veena came home after showing him the place. "Guess what, Beyji?. Do you know about his education? He is a B.A. pass, Beyji," she said with a look of pride on her face.

"Liar!" Maya responded with a smile.

"I swear, Beyji. I read it on his wallet."

"What was written on his wallet?"

"It said, 'Kedar Nath, B.A.'."

"Really!" Maya exclaimed. "He seems such a simple fellow. Has none of the airs that men with a B.A. degree put on these days!"

"Shall I go and clean up his room?" Veena inquired and left with a broom in hand without waiting for a reply.

CHAPTER 7

"*Shall* I tell you something, Beyji?"

"What?"

"Masterji sometimes starts crying while he is teaching me."

"Starts crying?"

"Yes, Beyji."

"Don't be silly!"

"Really, Beyji. I have spotted him crying on several occasions."

"But why? What could be the reason?"

"Who knows?"

"Why didn't you ask him the reason?"

"Me? Beyji, I myself feel like crying when I see him like that."

"Idiot! I am sure you said something that made him cry."

"I swear upon the Goddess, Beyji. I have never said anything like that. I was talking about Bhapaji, and he began to cry. He was trying his best to hide it from me but I'm not all that naïve. Why would his eyes get red if he wasn't crying?"

"Ask him! Find out why he cries."

"I have tried to find out more than once. But he always manages to change the subject."

"Has he left for the shop?"

"When I left his place, he was still at home. But he might have left by now."

"Why don't you go and call him. I might be able to find out what's wrong."

"Fine," Veena said and ran off towards his place.

It was now little over a month that Kedar had been working at Sardar Attar Singh's shop. In this short time, he had pleased his employer to such an extent that he had been handed over virtually full responsibility for running the shop. His honesty, hard work and intelligence had impressed Attar Singh to the point that he had even given him charge of the shop's keys. Kedar would earn as much as four or five rupees a day by repairing watches and would diligently hand over the entire amount each evening to his employer. What does a blind man want but two eyes! Where would Attar Singh get an employee who would pay him a rupee for every quarter that he received? As he entered his second month, Attar Singh himself felt obliged to raise Kedar's salary from twenty-five rupees to forty rupees a month.

Living next door to Panna Lal's place, Kedar soon became a part of their family. Every week or so, he would write a letter on Panna Lal's behalf and bring it to Maya.

"Here's a letter from him," he would say and proceed to read it out. The letters would contain whatever he thought the family would want to know. He was careful, though, to read out the letters only after making sure that Veena was not around. He suspected that Veena was bound to know what her father's handwriting looked like.

Veena was weak in math and needed a tutor but financial hardship had prevented her father from engaging one. Kedar took this responsibility upon himself, spending an hour every morning and an hour in the evening to teach her.

He was teaching Veena in his room that morning when she started chatting about her father. She said, "Masterji, you had said that you would only stay here till Bhapaji returns. But I will ask Bhapaji not to let you go. Would you not agree to his request?"

Kedar felt a strong surge of emotion as Veena chatted eagerly about her father. His eyes were brimming with tears and when Veena stopped talking and looked up at him, his resistance collapsed. Despite his best effort, he found himself unable to conceal his tears. Seeing him in this condition, Veena not only forgot about her lesson but herself broke into tears. After a while, Kedar tried to resume the lesson but Veena would have none of it. Like an obstinate child, she insisted on knowing the reason for his tears, while Kedar kept trying to dodge her queries.

Not making any headway, Veena finally gave up. Gathering her books, she said that she would go and tell Beyji, who would have her own way of getting to the bottom of the matter. Kedar's pleas that she must not tell her fell on deaf ears and Veena spoke to her mother about the incident as soon as she entered her home. Maya despatched Veena to fetch Kedar and she left immediately for his place.

After sending Veena off to bring Kedar, Maya started wondering why he should be crying. Could he be missing his home? He isn't all that old, after all. Or maybe, like us it is financial difficulties or some other major adversity that is bothering him. Her train of thought had not travelled much further than this when Veena entered the door, tugging Kedar by his arm.

"You wanted to see me, Bibiji?" Kedar inquired, feigning ignorance.

"Yes. I asked Veena to see if you could come."

"Is there anything I can do?"

"Why don't you sit for a while?" she said as Veena brought a stool for him.

"There is no time to sit right now, Bibiji. I must go to the shop," Kedar remained standing and said.

"Don't worry about that," Maya said in an affectionate tone that decisively established her claim on his time. "It won't take long."

"Tell me, then" he sat down and said.

"You know," Maya began, wondering how she should broach the topic. "You didn't complete Veena's lesson today? She hardly spent any time at all."

"Why don't you ask her? I told her to stay but she left her studies and ran off."

"What else could I have done?" Veena grasped the opening and said. "Once you started crying, who was going to teach me?"

Kedar found himself getting trapped into just the sort of situation that he was attempting to escape. Seeing his embarrassed look, Maya inquired gently, "Bharaji is that true or is she just making it up?"

"I am ready to bet a hundred rupees that it's true. I have seen it a couple of times before as well. You've been on the verge of tears while teaching me," Veena interjected before he could respond

Not seeing any escape route, Kedar admitted, "I did cry."

"But why?" Maya probed.

"Nothing. Just like that."

It can't be *nothing*. You have to tell me, Bharaji."

"I was missing my mother a lot," Kedar responded, unable to conjure a better excuse. Maya also refrained from repeating her query.

Maya had heard him mention about his mother's death on earlier occasions too. She heaved a deep sigh and said, "You are right, Bharaji. There is nothing in this world that can substitute one's parents. But when they leave, you have no choice but to accept it. There were times when Veena's Bhapaji would get overwhelmed by our problems and would say that he saw no point in remaining alive, that it would be better to die and escape this tortured existence. I would urge him not to talk in that fashion. Indeed, I would pray that my remaining years should also be added to his life. Everything in our home revolves around him. So what if we are passing through a difficult time, finding it hard to make both ends meet. At least the kids are safe in the knowledge that they have their parents' protective umbrella over their heads. But it's now been over a month since he left. This home has turned upside down. What a fine day it will be when he returns home safe and sound. Today, every minute is like an eternity. The kids also feel lost. They often wake up at night crying, 'Bhapaji! Bhapaji!'

Maya had called Kedar to probe into his sorrow but found that she had instead been carried away by her own misery. Each time she spoke wistfully about her husband, Kedar would feel a gut-wrenching tremor go through his own body, as though each sentence carried a hundred curses delivered to him by some unseen spirit. Maya was missing her husband, and Kedar alone knew that he might by now be the resident of another world and never again meet his unfortunate woman. He hated himself and felt his soul sinking under an immense burden. He found himself asking, 'How long will I deceive this ill-fated family? Am I not trying to cover the fire raging in their home under a bale of cotton? What fate awaits them when they learn the truth? Why don't I put an end to this deceit right now? Oh! Am I not the criminal who has orphaned these little kids? A criminal, and a fraudster too! May there be a curse on my very existence! Am I not like a snake hiding in this woman's robes? When she learns the truth and my reality stands exposed, her hatred will pierce every nerve in my body. The fire of her curses will burn my body to ashes. Oh God! Is there any atonement for my sins?'

Thoughts like these ran like a whirlwind through Kedar's head after hearing Maya's words. Sitting before her, he felt like a criminal. Instead of blood, he thought he had acid running through his veins.

Kedar's eyes were brimming with tears.

"You are crying again?" Maya asked her as she finished speaking and looked at his face. There was no response from Kedar, but Maya concluded, 'Poor fellow. He must really be missing his mother. I wish I could be his mother and fill the void in his heart.'

Kedar lifted his eyes and tears streamed down his cheeks. Looking at him, her own eyes filled up. She grabbed Kedar's shoulder and comforted him, "Come on! Can anyone's parents stay with him forever?"

And what if I were to say the same words to Veena, to tell her 'Veena! Your father's killer is advising you that your parents don't stay with you for ever!' How would *she* feel about it? Kedar lifted his eyes higher to look towards Veena. No sooner did their eyes meet that he felt his eyes lower again, as though under the weight of some unseen burden. Instead of stopping, his tears started streaming out more rapidly.

Maya caught hold of his other shoulder as well, and pulling him towards her, said "You can consider me like your mother. Please don't cry."

Kedar found himself moved by her maternal touch, her caring words. Unknowingly, his hands went around her neck — the neck of another woman. His eyes were shut, his mind inquiring expectantly, 'Could you really be my mother?' His tears were flowing even faster.

Maya's own maternal instincts were now fully aroused. For a while, she forgot that Kedar was not her own offspring. She was now hugging him tight and also gently rubbing his back to comfort him. The two souls were coming closer, standing at the boundaries of unfamiliarity. Maya was now dominated by her sense of motherhood. Oblivious of any thought of sexuality, she had ascended to that summit of mother-son relationship where even the gods of the universe were bowing to her. She had gone beyond the position of a mere woman to take the form of womanhood itself, clutching somebody else's son to her bosom, a surge of nectar filling her breasts. She represented that awesome female power whose blessings can wash a thousand sins but whose curse can destroy the entire universe.

8080 NANAK SINGH

Kedar – the male child, son of the universal woman – had completely forgotten whose bosom was cradling him. Was it his mother, or was it a woman that he should not even be touching. Hugging her even tighter, his head nestling in Maya's bosom, he sobbed hysterically like a child and cried, 'Mother! Mother!'

Veena was watching this astonishing scene with growing wonderment, tears flowing down her own face. An unreal atmosphere permeated the room.

Eventually, the arms parted. Without uttering a word through her lips, Maya was saying, 'Kedar! Can't I fill the void left by your mother?"

And Kedar was also asking himself, 'She has her own children! Will she really be able to adopt this unfamiliar son?'

CHAPTER 8

$\mathscr{A}$ second month passed by, and then a third. Panna Lal had still not returned, and his family had by now reached the limits of its endurance. Using one pretext or another, Kedar had managed to keep them engaged but there is a point beyond which even lies refuse to be stretched. He would write letters regularly from Panna Lal to Maya offering detailed explanations for his inability to return just yet on account of all manner of complications but keeping her hopes alive with assurances that he would be coming back soon.

Worry about Panna Lal's fate had rendered his innards hollow like a log eaten away by termites. In his heart of hearts, he was sure that Panna Lal - as he had so clearly signalled in his letter – must already have taken his life. He also believed that he was responsible for taking Panna Lal's life and that the divine powers would subject him to a severe punishment for this sin.

Hoping against hope, he secretly placed advertisements in several newspapers to find Panna Lal, even offering financial rewards for information. None of these efforts had so far yielded results. There were times when he would think that Panna Lal might still be alive, but the question that stared him in the face was 'How does one find someone who has lost himself in this vast world?' And he would always come to the same unhappy conclusion, 'No. He must have gone to some distant place and taken his own life. How could a person as emotional and as unhappy as Panna Lal be alive, knowing as he did how his family would fare in his absence?'

To the casual observer, Kedar seemed to be leading a fairly comfortable and contented existence. He was receiving the fullest affection from Maya and her children. Veena, in particular, was getting increasingly attached to him. Most important, Maya had virtually become like a mother to him. To any stranger asking her, she would have replied that she had not two but three sons. As for Attar Singh, he had never been happier. Finding Kedar was like finding a gold mine. Thanks to Kedar, he was now making over hundred and fifty rupees a month from the repair of watches alone, and he had increased Kedar's salary by another ten rupees.

But did these trappings of comfort and goodwill mean that Kedar was happy? Was his mind at peace? If so, why was his colour getting pale by the day? Panna Lal's curse was still reverberating in his head in an ever louder and more terrifying pitch.

Every four or five days, Maya would get Veena to write a long letter to Panna Lal and give it to Kedar to post. Kedar would carefully add them to the pile that he had already accumulated in a weather-beaten aluminium trunk in his room. Each month, Kedar would retain just five rupees from his salary and give the rest to Maya with the words that this was Panna Lal's salary. But the complication about Veena's marriage stood where it was, and its strain was taking its toll on Maya.

Although Kedar nominally stayed at his own place, all his meals were at Panna Lal's house. He had recently suffered from an upset stomach and when Maya had learnt that the probable cause was the food he ate from the bazaar, she had insisted that Kedar must eat with them. Starting with the day that he had cried in Maya's presence, his association with the family had grown steadily and he was now like an integral a part of the household. He shared every secret of the family, except the one about Veena's engagement. This was the one thing that Maya had still not confided in him. She had often thought of telling Kedar everything so that she could inquire if Panna Lal had managed to raise the issue with Sardarji before leaving for Bombay. But she had been unable to summon the courage till now. Eventually, she could hold back no more and in the flow of conversation one day, she found herself speaking about it.

Kedar returned from the shop that evening and sat down in Maya's room. Maya had just finished putting her younger son to sleep, and Veena was in the kitchen. Kedar would usually drop into their house at this time and chat with Maya for a little while before going to his own place.

"Kedar! (That was how she addressed him now) May I ask you something?

"Please go ahead, Beyji. (He now used the maternal address *Beyji* instead of the more formal *Bibiji*).

"Will you reply truthfully?"

"As though I usually tell you lies, Beyji." But Kedar's heart sank. First, he had no clue what she was going to ask, and second, his heart asked him if he had ever spoken the truth before them.

"Why do you always remain so sad? What exactly is the cause of your worries?"

"Nothing, Beyji. When someone has a mother like you, what kind of worry could he possibly have?"

"Then why do you always look so despondent?"

"Not at all, Beyji. This is just your imagination. In fact, this is something that I have wanted to ask you. You are the one who keeps sighing sadly all the time. I've often thought of asking you but have been unable to."

"Unlike you, Kedar, I won't try to deny. It is true that my heart is weighed under a huge burden. I promise to share it with you, but first you must tell me about your problem."

"Believe me, Beyji. I have no problem."

"Kedar, aren't you like my son?"

Kedar twitched nervously. Maya's eyes were overflowing with affection as he looked into them and said, "If Kedar gets the feeling that Beyji no longer considers him her son, he will be unable to spend another minute in this world."

"Heaven forbid that such a time should ever come," Maya said as she hugged Kedar to her bosom in much the same fashion that she had done that first day. "Honestly, Kedar, you must tell me what is bothering you," she repeated.

"Nothing at all, Beyji. Nothing at all! Please get this misconception out of your mind," he said. But his whole frame trembled, as though he was trying to lift a weight several times larger than his capacity.

"Then why are you getting weaker by the day? Tell me, Kedar, have I not given you the same love that you were getting from your mother?"

"Come on, Beyji. No mother can love a son more."

"Stop lying, Kedar. If that were the case, you would have forgotten the sorrow of your mother's loss by now."

"What are you saying, Beyji? How can this question arise when my own mother has come back to me from the heavens? Who says she has died? My mother...my mother is with me," Kedar said as he buried his head in Maya's bosom.

Maya was not convinced but she told herself that in an emotionally overwrought situation like this, none could lie, let alone a sensitive soul like Kedar. Nay, that was well nigh impossible. Reluctantly, she accepted that he must be telling the truth.

"Now it's your turn to speak, Beyji," Kedar said with a touch of nervousness.

As Maya spoke, her words started to sweep Kedar into the vortex of a hurricane. His already unhealthy complexion seemed to turn a ghastly pale.

Unburdening her intolerable pain on Kedar, Maya said, "Our family has enjoyed a noble reputation over seven generations. People would use our name as a guarantee. But fate dealt us such a cruel blow that within days everything went up in smoke. Veena's father lost his self-esteem the day we received the letter of rejection from her in-laws. To save the situation, I came up with the plan that he should approach Sardarji for some assistance so that we might salvage our honour. But he left for Bombay that very day, and nothing materialised. Although there is no real reason to be optimistic about a positive response from Veena's in-laws, I fear that I will be constantly plagued by the thought that if only I had visited them once, pleaded before them, maybe they would have relented. Until now, we have managed to keep this matter under wraps. But if word gets out in our community, I will be unable to show my face anywhere."

Kedar felt the blood freeze in his arteries. Seeing the despondent expression on Maya's face, he said, "So why didn't you visit them, Beyji? No harm in making the effort."

Despite her gloomy state, Maya managed a laugh, "You can be really naïve at times, Kedar. On what basis do I visit them?"

"So you think they are turning down the marriage because they fear that the dowry might be inadequate?"

"That's precisely why I sent Veena's father to Sardarji that day. But we have never had the chance to discuss it thereafter. A couple of times I gave him an oblique reminder in my letters but he said nothing in his response."

Kedar's brain scanned the letters that Veena had written for Maya and given him to post to Panna Lal. He now remembered a couple of phrases. 'Did you get any response from Sardarji…. Have you managed to arrange something for that matter…' It dawned on Kedar that Maya had deliberately coded her messages so that Veena should not learn about the real nature of the matter.

Feeling a surge of empathy for Maya's burdens, Kedar said, "Tell me, Beyji! How much do you think is required to deal with this situation?"

Maya heaved a long sigh and said, "What can I say, Kedar? Boys' parents these days want the girl's side to hand over its house and hearth to them. But our financial situation is such that it's a daily struggle to make both ends meet. Whatever we offer will be inadequate but at the very least we must have a thousand or twelve hundred rupees for the marriage. That is why I told Veena's father that I am willing to sell whatever meagre jewellery I have and if we can supplement it with a loan of five or seven hundred rupees from Sardarji, we might be able to save our honour." Maya let out another deep sigh, as though it was the only way she could give vent to her woes.

"In that case, Beyji," Kedar said with an unexpectedly cheerful note, "You should plan an early trip to Gujarkhan. I am sure that I will be able to arrange this amount."

Kedar's words miraculously lifted the enormous weight that was crushing Maya. She lifted her eyes to gaze at Kedar and parted her lips to say something. But overcome by sheer affection and gratitude, they failed to utter a sound. Her eyes, now somewhat moist, conveyed what her words could not, and lowered again. Kedar did not need to look at her face to gauge her feelings. His attention, instead, was focussed on that barren expanse of his life where he could discern a slight glimmer of hope in the distance even as he sensed a gust building up faraway, threatening to come towards him at such speed that it would surely blow out the little glimmer.

Chapter 9

$\mathcal{M}$aya left for Gujarkhan that morning and after seeing her off, Veena went to Kedar's room at the usual time. She normally spent an hour studying with him each morning.

By this time, Kedar would usually have finished his bath and would be waiting for her. But when Veena arrived today, she found him still in bed, with the covers drawn over his face.

"Bharaji," she called, having now started addressing him with the sister's term for a brother instead of the pupil's *Masterji*. Kedar heard the voice and abruptly sat up in his bed. Veena glanced at his furrowed countenance and bloodshot eyes and immediately felt a twinge of fear. "What's wrong?" she asked.

Kedar let out a huge yawn and, clutching the sheet around him, asked "Has Beyji gone?"

"Yes. She just left," Veena sat beside him and said. "I asked you something."

"It's nothing. Just a bit of a headache....Will Beyji be back in the evening?"

"I don't know."

"Don't know? Who would know if you don't?"

"Maybe you should know."

"Me? Don't be silly! She's gone for *your* work and *I* am the one who should know?"

Veena blushed and lowered her eyes. Kedar felt that some of the nerves in his forehead were getting entangled with each other.

"Anyway, please start the lesson," Veena opened her school bag and said. "I am already getting late for school. Vidya doesn't want to get out of bed till it is high noon and I have been up since dawn. Started with cleaning the courtyard, then made the beds, prepared a meal for Beyji and saw her off. I've just finished giving the kids a bath, though I haven't had a chance yet to comb my own hair. I thought I should first get you to explain some of the geometry problems and also get you to take a look at yesterday's translation work," Veena said and unconsciously started to move her palm over her head to fix her hair.

Kedar began explaining the geometry problems but found that he was making a complete mess.

"Why Bharaji?" Veena asked when she heard a cold sigh emanate nearby and again glanced at Kedar's drawn face and downcast expression. "What's the matter with you today?"

"Nothing," he replied as he tried to take control of himself.

"Fine! Don't say anything. Why should I care anyway?" Veena pouted with a hurt expression. His silence worried her, leading her to repeat her query. Failing once again to elicit any response, she threw down her book and, tugging insistently at his hand, asked again, "So you won't tell?"

"How does it matter if I don't?" Kedar set aside the geometry book and complained. "Haven't you always treated me like a stranger?"

"Me?" Veena leaned her head against his shoulder and asked. "Are you really saying this from your heart?"

"Of course."

"Okay! I am never going to speak with you again," Veena said and started to gather her books. As she knelt to pick up the book from the floor, Kedar caught her arm and pulled her beside him, saying, "If you didn't consider me a stranger, you would have responded to my question."

"What question?" Veena again sat by his side and asked. She had no idea what he was asking about.

"What I had asked earlier…. When will Beyji be back?"

"Come on, now! There's nothing to that."

"There is something. That's why I asked, and that's why you have not responded."

"Will it make you happy if I told you?"

"Yes."

"She will return tomorrow morning by the 10:30 train. She said the 7 PM train only arrives around 10 in the night and it would be an unnecessary bother to take that. So? I hope you are not angry any more? Such a minor thing. Even I could have figured out that she wouldn't return tonight because the night train gets in very late."

"I just wanted do know why she has gone to Gujarkhan?" Kedar said, once again feeling his nerves tying themselves into knots. Seeing that Veena had lowered her gaze, Kedar again unleashed a taunting arrow. "Now you know why I said that you treat me like an outsider."

"Do you know," Veena gripped his arm and said, "By saying this, you are being completely unfair to me? But….Bharaji? What is this? Why are you trembling?"

"Who…me?" Kedar closed his eyes and gently freed his arm from her grasp.

For several minutes, neither of them uttered a word, though their eyes remained transfixed on each other.

"What!" Veena exclaimed with a mixture of fear and surprise as she held his hand again. "Bharaji, you are not making any sense today. And your eyes…see how they look!"

"How do they look?"

"Sort of scary."

'Are my eyes really creating some kind of doubt in Veena's mind?' Kedar asked himself as he got up from the bed and meandered around the room. "I am not feeling well today, Veena. I have a splitting headache. Let us leave the studies till the evening." But his heart was still directing all kinds of questions at Veena. 'Are you really keen to get married?…What if your in-laws refuse to accept you?…What if your mother returns disappointed?…What if…if…if…' But he found himself unable to pose these queries to Veena.

As she was leaving, Veena said, "You take a bath and get dressed now. I'll make a cup of tea and ask Vidya to bring it to you. That should make you feel a bit better. But if you don't feel up to it, don't go for work today. If you want, I could ask Basant to go to the shop and let them know."

"Don't worry. It's not all that bad. But sure, send a cup of tea," Kedar said and went towards the bathroom as Veena collected her books and left.

A tremor of fear ran through Kedar when he came out of the bathroom and looked at his face in the mirror. He felt that he was staring at the face of a dead man. Swiftly turning away from the mirror, he dressed up in a hurry and departed from his home. He left the door ajar, forgetting to close it as he went.

When he reached the shop, he hoped that pre-occupation with work would set his mind at rest but as the day went by, his discomfort only increased further.

He was sitting at the worktable where he repaired watches. He opened up one watch and cleaned its components but before he could start putting it together again, he felt that the components of his own heart were being scattered around him. He was

searching for answers within himself. 'Am I a sinner?' Not just a sinner but also double-crossing and selfish. When I have already called Maya my mother, can her daughter be anything but a sister to me? Did I enter their home as a thief, to steal their treasures? To destroy someone's life?'

'Veena! Why is she capturing my senses in this fashion? Do I desire her? Do I love her? But – what kind of effect is this love having on me? Does love carry a fire within itself? If not, why does the thought of Veena set afire every nerve in my body – with a taste that is sharp, yet sweet. It is a kind of insanity, this burning sensation. Why? Is this the effect of love? Then, love must surely burn a man to ashes pretty quickly. Oh! I wish someone could explain these mysteries to me. If this is love, surely it will finish me off soon. They say that love is God. Is it God that burns you? Is it God that tests you? If God lives within love, would love carry these unseemly stains, like tell-tale signs left behind by a fire? No, that is not possible. Either love is not God, or if love really is God then what I understand to be love is not love at all but something else.' Lost in these thoughts, Kedar would get a multitude of feelings arising within him like small gusts of wind which would suddenly acquire the dimensions of a dangerous storm, scattering his random thoughts in every direction until an unseen force would pull Kedar and transport him to another place.

He was taken far away – unknown to him, so far that he had gone beyond his own control – where he not only could not catch himself but where he was almost afraid to catch himself, as one would be afraid to catch a rabid dog. Several times, he made abortive attempts to retrieve himself but he had now reached a place from where return was not just unlikely but virtually unheard of. He spent several hours in this twilight zone.

Unable to concentrate on his work, Kedar gathered the scattered components of the watches and left for his home after telling the proprietor that he was not feeling well. Kedar's ashen face and sagging frame provided such strong evidence of his condition that the proprietor did not even deem it necessary to inquire into the nature or extent of his illness.

As he entered his street and turned towards his home, he again tried to investigate his condition. From head to toe, he felt himself burning. His feet were turning the ground below to smouldering block. His mind had been emptied of every thought except one that obsessively repeated itself over and over again. 'Veena is alone at home today.'

He was now before his house. The door that he had left ajar in the morning had now been bolted. For a short moment, his feet dragged him to the entrance of the house a little further down – Veena's house.

It was almost noon on a hot summer day but Kedar's insides were shivering as though he had just been pulled out of a blizzard.

Under the rosewood tree in front of their house, Vidya was playing with a couple of her friends. Seeing Kedar, she ran towards him and cried, "Bharaji, you left this morning without having tea and you also left your door open."

Kedar did not seem to hear her. In a quivering voice, he asked, "Where is Veena?"

"In the kitchen."

"What is she doing?"

"Must be washing the dishes. Come and have your meal."

"No, I am not hungry."

Vidya resumed playing with her friends, and Kedar stood there thinking, 'Where am I going? If I don't want to eat and I am not feeling well, why have I come towards Veena's house?' These thoughts awakened his sense of reasoning, which had been momentarily overcome by his emotions and he heard the questions reverberate inside him with a rising tempo 'Where am I going? Why? For what purpose?' And he found his feet make an abrupt retreat.

He was once again before his own house. He opened the door and entered in a hurry, lest he collapse before getting inside. He felt his head swim and his eyes become misty, as though enveloped by a dense fog.

A pot of tea and a cup and saucer sat on the table. He poured himself a cup of the cold tea and quickly drank it at one go. Bolting the door from inside, still wearing his shoes, he lay down on his bed. For a while, he lay motionless, as though in a semi-conscious state, forgetting about himself and his condition. But this self-delusion did not last too long and he soon started feeling as though his head and heart had exchanged places.

He was in a surreal state, at the borders of the place where sin and virtue, religion and impiety, and peace and violence begin to overlap. He felt himself perched precariously on the narrow wall of dilemma from where even a small gust of wind could have toppled him.

The paths of compassion and wickedness usually take opposing directions. Unsuspecting travellers go their own ways on each path. But think of the plight of a person like Kedar who has one foot on the path of compassion while the other is trying to take him down the road of wickedness.

Each time he saw Veena's face before his eyes, each time thoughts about her revolved in his mind, each time her voice rang in his ears, Kedar would feel himself getting lost, oscillating between the fountain of nectar and the cesspool of poison.

He found himself entertaining ideas that could only be described as sure signs of insanity. Sometimes, he would be intoxicated by the charms of her presence to the point that he could almost feel an electric current traversing his body. At other times, he would see his susceptibility as proof of his own cowardice and timidity. But then, his heart would cry out and say, 'I cannot live without Veena – she alone can save me.' At which point another element entered his train of thought – 'I hope Veena's mother does not succeed in her mission in Gujarkhan, so that…' And then the blindly flowing currents would come to an abrupt halt and reverse their direction. Thoughts of Veena's sisterly affection and concern for him, and the deep vulnerability of her situation would spin him around completely. For a while, his eyes would light up as he savoured the pleasant thoughts. But anger at the actions of his evil mind would surface soon, leaving him restive and agitated once again. He wanted to fly away to another world far away, where a pure soul like Veena could not even be touched by his unclean shadow.

'Would Veena ever forgive me if she knows my real intentions?' This question would keep turning over in his head. He continued to agonise over his dilemma. 'What if she finds out? Would she curse me? Or would she be ready to feed my lust? And if she does not agree?' Morality and Lust – one after the other, each would come to lecture Kedar on its point of view and Kedar would find himself first facing one and turning his back to the other and then reversing his position to listen to the earlier one.

The persistent lecturing by the opposing streams left Kedar feeling so troubled and uneasy that he could neither turn around on his side nor get up from his bed.

Kedar thought he was on the verge of losing his sanity. He felt an inexplicable impulse to lash out and destroy himself and the whole world. Like some murderous beast, his eyes glowed like embers. He was now certain that he had gone stark, raving mad. He wanted to dash out into the street, rip his clothes apart and charge into any bystander, crushing himself and the bystander to bits.

Unexpectedly, he heard someone knocking the door. He got up with a start and shouted, "Who is it?"

"Its me, Veena." Kedar felt an explosion go off inside his chest. He got up but because of the semi-darkness inside and because his own senses seemed to have dimmed, he found himself disoriented and unable to establish the exact direction from which the sound was coming. But it did not take him long to know whose voice it was.

After a short interval, the voice called again. Kedar was now standing near the door. His room appeared like a giant furnace to him and from head to toe, he looked like a lunatic who wanted to crush the entire world beneath his feet.

"Please open the door, Bharaji," the sweet voice pleaded once again.

"Get lost. I am nobody's brother," Kedar said, now virtually out of control.

"Bharaji...Bharaji."

"Get lost. Go away from here, I say!"

"Bharaji...you...you..."

"What is this 'you...you.' Haven't I told you to go away immediately?" Kedar yelled so loudly that his voice was cracking.

Kedar threw his body back on the bed as though it was a lifeless sack. His ears, though, were straining to hear if he might catch the same voice again. But this time, not a whisper came his way.

He was now desperate to hear Veena's voice again, even though he had just abused her. He thought, 'She must have come to call me for dinner. And what did *I* do? Oh! What a disgrace!'

Kedar was like a drowning man whose head was completely submerged and who was now drawing his last gasps of air — like one who has given up all hope of life and wants to die but life is refusing to leave him.

He spent the entire day in this condition. After some time, he heard someone knocking the door again. He heard voices, 'Bharaji...open the door.' He recognised Basant's voice and stubbornly remained in his bed.

The day went by, and night enveloped the world in its dark blanket. As time passed, the storms raging inside Kedar gathered strength. He could no longer see anything inside the room. His mind was spinning out of control, like a twig adrift in a whirlpool. Caught in the vortex of a swift and powerful current, he drifted for hours until he reached a place that is beyond the pale of intelligence or reason, where the overpowering torrents choke the human spirit before contemptuously tossing it aside as unconscious or half dead, where the boundaries between man and beast begin to merge, where the distinctions between friends and strangers, between truth and fiction begin to evaporate.

He spent half the night in this condition. Then, without warning, he yanked himself out of the bed and went upstairs to the terrace. Why and for what purpose? Perhaps he knew but yet did not know.

In the middle of the night, in pitch dark, Kedar was pacing up and down on the terrace. In a tall building standing in the distance, a sliver of light escaped from a window to draw a dim line in the darkness. Kedar's eyes swept across the horizon and came to a rest at Panna Lal's house and in his imagination, he could see the still outline of Veena sleeping on their rooftop terrace. A shiver ran through him and soon, he felt his eyes burn and his heart pound against his chest with the power of a blacksmith's hammer. The thought that Veena's mother was not home tonight returned to his mind and with trembling legs, he started walking towards the terrace of Panna Lal's house.

Panna Lal's house was adjacent to his, with just a short wall separating the roof of the two houses. Kedar crossed this with one leap and found himself on Panna Lal's terrace. His entire body was quivering with tension.

He saw two beds before him, with Veena sleeping on one and her younger siblings on the other. For a while, he found himself rooted to his position, unable to will his legs to move. A voice deep inside him called, 'Kedar! What are you about to do? In which direction are you going?' He retreated a few steps, then paused. Another voice was ordering him, "You fool! How can you retreat when you have come so close? Why are you subjecting yourself to this slow torture? Move forward!'

He moved a few steps. A dog barked in the street. He felt that someone was standing behind him, carefully observing his actions – someone who was treading softly in his shadows, standing so close that he could almost hear him breathe.

Kedar was gasping with fear. He turned around to look behind but saw no one. It was just his imagination. The footsteps he heard were his own, as was the breathing.

Kedar felt himself tumbling down from outer space towards some bottomless pit. He shut his eyes in fear and found some power inside him once again propelling him towards Veena's bed.

Inching forward, he crept up to Veena's bedside. He could feel his entire frame on fire. His eyes were riveted on Veena's still form as she lay face down, one hand under her chest and the other near her head. One side of her olive green dupatta hung over the side of the bed. In the darkness of the night, it appeared black and part of it gently cascaded over her limbs, which glistened in the dark like the moon of some lonely planet.

Sub-consciously, or perhaps knowingly, Kedar sat down on the floor besides the bed where he was earlier standing. His hand was gently caressing her plaited hair.

Once again, a voice inside him asked, 'Kedar! Kedar! What are you doing?' He heard the voice but ignored it.

He stood up, tiptoed around her bed and softly eased himself down on its wooden frame. His gaze was transfixed on Veena's face and his eyes were feasting themselves on her delicate features. He sat absolutely still, not even daring to breathe. Veena gently stretched herself and turned over on her side. She now had her back towards him.

Kedar waited for a while before quietly getting up and silently moving to the other side of the bed. Feeling a lot braver, he sat down besides Veena, his body almost touching hers. Not satisfied with this, he placed a trembling hand on Veena's shoulder and then quickly retracted it. He apprehended that Veena had perhaps sensed his actions because he had felt a little tremble when his hand had touched her shoulder. But he realised that this was again a creation of his imagination; it was his own hand that was trembling.

Veena moved once again. Her arm, earlier lying on her side, came to a rest on Kedar's knee. A tremor ran through Kedar's body. He felt his blood was on fire and its flames were searing his insides as they rose towards his head.

Moving slowly, he placed his hand on Veena's. He was now holding her hand, gently caressing it when Veena suddenly jerked it away.

Veena's eyelashes moved and her eyes gradually opened. Discerning Kedar's form in the dark, her eyes fluttered rapidly in astonishment as she exclaimed, "Bharaji! You?"

CHAPTER 10

*R*andom thoughts were rapidly churning around in Veena's head, like a top that is spinning at a high speed but appears to be stationary, like the rapidly moving frames of a reel that are brought to a halt when they appear as images in a cinema. She had no idea how much of the night had elapsed. Lying on her bed and gazing at the clear sky above her, she was thinking of the day's events.

Going to Kedar's place in the morning, she had found that unlike most days, he was still in bed. She had assumed that Kedar might be suffering from one of his frequent headaches. But his disjointed speech, his apparent disinterest in what he was teaching and the expression of turmoil writ large on his face suggested that his pain was mental as much as it was physical. She desperately wanted Kedar to unlock the secrets of his heart to her, to not keep anything hidden. But she felt inhibited when he started asking her questions that hinted at her own marriage. 'Why was Kedar asking these questions,' she kept thinking. 'And why did he stop before he had said anything.' She was keen to probe further into these questions but found herself unable to summon the necessary courage.

After he had asked her to get some tea and had gone off to get dressed for work, Veena wanted to wait and make another attempt to find out what was wrong. But Kedar seemed to be in a hurry to go to the shop and she too had to go to her school. Deciding to leave the issue for another time, she went back to her kitchen to make tea for him. As she sat in front of the stove and waited for the water to boil, she found her thoughts again being pulled in the same direction. She asked Vidya to take the tea for him and when Vidya returned to say that Kedar had left without having the tea, she felt even more perplexed.

Pouring herself a cup of the remaining tea from the pan, she had a sip and was surprised to discover that she had forgotten to add sugar. She instantly concluded that Kedar did not have the tea because it was so tasteless. She decided to skip school and began to wait impatiently for Kedar to return.

Right through that morning, Veena's mind was preoccupied with two thoughts – about Kedar, and about her in-laws. Veena was acutely aware of the errand that had carried her mother to Gujarkhan. She felt that the golden dreams of her future were closely tied to the success of her mother's visit.

'What if they decline the marriage?' Whenever she asked herself this small question, she felt her dreams collapsing around her. She would then remind herself that Kedar had committed himself to honouring her in-laws demands and there was no longer any reason for them to decline. This would send her spirits soaring and she would find herself amidst the images sketched out by Channo during the course of their many conversations. 'He is truly handsome…sings so sweetly…the water from their well…and garden…and large houses…'

'Where will Kedar get all that money?' This would again raise some doubts in her mind, until she would reassure herself with the thought that he has made a promise; surely he will find a way of meeting his commitment. And she would find her heart swept away by a wave of emotion as she thought of his kindness and generosity.

'I hope he isn't feeling too unwell!' Veena thought with growing concern when he did not turn up for lunch. She fed her brothers and sisters and cleaned up the kitchen but did not feel like eating anything. Several times, she went herself or asked her siblings to go and see if he had returned but found his door locked. She told Vidya to play near the rosewood tree and keep an eye out for him. After a long wait, Vidya came in to inform her that Kedar had come to their door and asked about her but declined to enter and left soon thereafter. Veena quickly changed her clothes, combed her hair and went towards his house.

Finding his door bolted from inside, Veena knocked and then called out for him. The response that she received from inside was completely contrary to her expectations. She could not believe her ears. His harsh words came like a bolt from the blue to her gentle disposition. Unwilling to believe that it was Kedar's voice, she made another effort and called again. The response came in the same tone and manner and she found herself unable to stand there any longer. For a while, she did consider that she could plead at the door and try to ask Kedar about the reason for his anger and offer evidence of her own innocence. But her own sense of pride and self-respect intervened to say, 'Who does he think he is to insult me like this? Am I a little child that I can be scolded this way? Why should I appeal for kindness, and for what fault?'

With these thoughts, Veena turned back to her house. Going straight to her bed, she lay face down and wept uncontrollably, her tears gradually drenching her pillow. She could not comprehend what had hit her.

There is no pain as bad as the pain of humiliation – especially the humiliation of one whose heart is full of love for someone. Amidst her sobbing, Veena kept searching, 'Why did he slight me like this? What harm have I done to him?' The thought then came to her mind, 'I hope he is not mad. May be he was speaking in a semi-conscious state. Or perhaps he was speaking like that because he was suffering from high fever or some other great pain. Otherwise, how can someone like Kedar speak in such anger? One hasn't even seen a frown crease his brow. Must be something unusual, otherwise...' Leaving her thoughts incomplete, she got up from her bed. The embers ignited by the sense of insult had cooled somewhat. She called Basant and asked him to check if Kedar's door was open or still closed from inside.

Basant came back and informed, "The door is bolted from inside. I knocked at the door and also called but nobody responded."

'I hope he isn't lying unconscious,' Veena thought and set off for his house. But seeing three women chatting near his door, she halted her steps. 'What would the neighbours say? Mother's not at home and look at her going again and again to his house, knocking at the door and yelling out for him,' she told herself and returned to her home.

Veena did not eat anything that evening either.

Evening gave way to night, and to bedtime. Veena made both beds on the terrace, giving one to her siblings and lying down on the other one. Normally, she would fall asleep as soon as she hit the bed but sleep simply refused to come anywhere near her eyes tonight. It was a hot summer night, and there was no breeze at all. She would ask herself, 'How can he sleep inside his room on a hot and sultry night like this? I hope he isn't...' The thought jerked her up from the bed and her feet began to move involuntarily down the steps. But three or four steps down, she thought, 'What would someone say...in the middle of the night...in pitch dark...' She returned to her bed to lie down once again.

Veena's eyes were fixed on the millions of twinkling stars in the sky above her. She was looking at the Milky Way as it wound its uneven path across the skies, its far end gradually widening until it seemed to merge with the multitudes of stars. 'How does the sky hold these countless numbers of stars? And where does this hazy, white road lead to?' she wondered. In the distance, she heard a train's whistle. She started thinking, 'Where would Beyji be at this time? Maybe at their house? No. How could she sleep in *their* house? In a sensitive relationship like this, that's impossible. She would probably have gone to some other relative's place. In fact, Bhapaji's elder brother's son lives in the same town. She must have gone to their house. After all, how can one sleep at the in-laws place?

'But why did she have to visit them? What petition of mercy has she taken to them? To plead that they must accept her daughter? Oh! Why must she accept this kind of humiliation? Would it be such a great accomplishment if she manages to persuade them at the cost of her own pride and self-respect? What had they written in that letter – 'our son does not yet want to get married.' So is it Veena who is so anxious to get married? Alas! I wish my mother had taken the time to learn my own views about this. I would have told her straight away what I thought of such arrogant people. I would rather remain unmarried all my life, but...'

Her meandering train of thought once again carried her to memories of Channo's words: 'He really loves you a lot…Always asks me about you…' At this point, her train abruptly changed its course and she told herself, 'No. This mischief must be entirely his parents' doing. They probably want to get the highest possible price for their son. How can the poor fellow be blamed for all this?' Veena would now see herself in an entirely different world, a world in which she was bedecked in diamonds and jewellery and sequined bridal dresses. She could almost feel the henna on her hands, a row of wedding bangles made from ivory coming all the way up to her elbows, and a Shikarpuri gold stud in her nose.

She blinked her eyes. The Milky Way had become brighter because the crescent shaped moon, which had so far dimmed the stars with its own brilliance, had completed its duty for the evening and travelled beyond the horizon. It was pitch dark all around her. As soon as she blinked her eyes, the imaginary world that she had created around her vanished instantly. She looked at her hands and arms as though she actually expected to find something on them. She looked around her and imagined that she could see Kedar's room in the darkness. She saw Kedar inside the room, his face covered by a sheet and his body drenched in sweat and thought she was remembering a scene that she had seen years ago. 'What? He is still inside his room, in this oppressive heat!' She sat up again in her bed, but returned to the pillow without even getting off the bed. Somewhere in the distance, a clock sounded the twelve strokes of midnight. Veena felt something gnawing inside her and wondered if she might be hungry. Her mind again started going over the events of the day as they had unfolded. She had eaten nothing since morning. She turned her eyes towards the sky but found herself unable to focus either on the stars or even on the Milky Way. She started looking at the glimmering stars with a strange sort of fear that made her lower her eyes. Her eyelids felt increasingly heavy.

Flying through the world of dreams, Veena's mind soon arrived at the place where so many of her future aspirations had taken the form of a strong, handsome and caring man who now appeared before her. She was in that world which lies at the border of maidenhood and married life and is known as the wedding night. She could feel the clinking of the ivory wedding bangles in her arms, the Shikarpuri stud in her nose and the deep colour of henna on her palms. A tray laden with all manner of sweets and exotic fruits beside her. She was eating some of her favourite delicacies with great relish and also feeding them to someone sitting near her. She then found herself in a garden full of beautiful flowers. A well nearby provided water that glistened like a silver ribbon as it flowed towards the plants. Veena was on a swing under a large mango tree. She was sitting with someone who would pluck a mango from a high branch each time the swing went up. He would present the mango to Veena, who would start eating it with evident pleasure.

When the swing came to a standstill, Veena saw herself sitting in the garden, surrounded by flowers. Her companion would go to pluck a flower and tuck it into her winding plait. At some distance, hiding behind the mango tree, she could spy her friend Channo who would briefly poke her head out to cast a knowing look and smile before disappearing behind the tree. Veena was both irritated and pleased by her intrusion.

Veena's companion was sitting by her side, easing the wedding veil off her face so that he could peer into her eyes and say, "Will this moon always remain hidden behind clouds?" Veena blushed and replied demurely, "Come on, now. Beyji must be waiting for me. I am sure she would not have eaten without me, and I too am feeling hungry."

"I won't let you leave until you remove this veil," he said and clasped Veena's hand. Veena was trying to pull her hand out of his grasp and the ensuing struggle broke her reverie. She opened her eyes but found no trace of the world that she had just left. Except that her hand was in somebody's hand. Opening her eyes wider, she looked carefully at the figure sitting next to her. Recognition dawned upon her and she said, "Bharaji! Was it you?"

Her words were like a splash of cool water on Kedar's burning soul, bringing him out of his deep trance. He could now feel himself, and feel the gravity of the act that he had just committed. Veena's eyes were wide open, staring at him in disbelief. He quickly got up from the bed and wanted to immediately make a dash for safety. But what would Veena think? The realisation held him back.

Veena also set up and, shaking his arm, asked, "What's wrong, Bharaji? Are you feeling all right? Why are you becoming like this?"

"I was feeling very dizzy," Kedar clasped his head with both hands and said in a trembling voice. He had lowered his eyes.

"Feeling dizzy?" Veena asked with concern. "Come, let me take you downstairs." She put her arm around his waist to provide him support and gingerly began to take him down the steps.

"Lie down for a while," she said as she took him into the room and helped him sit on the bed. "Are you feeling better now?" she switched on the light and asked.

"No," Kedar said, his hands still clutching his head. Veena held him by the shoulders and pushed him back so that he could lie down. Sitting beside him, she began to gently massage his forehead. She could see beads of cold sweat forming on his head and was getting increasingly nervous. She got up from the bed and aimlessly went around the room, not quite sure what she was looking for.

Returning to Kedar's side with growing anxiety, she looked at him closely. She could see that he was breathing quickly and his heart also seemed to be thumping at an alarmingly rapid rate. His eyes were shut and his lips were partly open. Perspiration was dripping from his body. Veena held a small fan in one hand to provide some cooling even as her other hand massaged his forehead.

"Are you okay, Bharaji?" Veena looked at his face and asked again. His lips were speechless and all she could get out of him was a grunt that seemed to come out of the back of his throat.

Veena was now extremely tense. She was rapidly massaging his head, shoulders and arms and repeatedly inquiring, "Bharaji...Bharaji...are you feeling any better? I was already concerned that you are not well today. God! What a mistake I made by not going back to check on you."

After quite a while, Kedar opened his eyes. Veena was vigorously massaging his arms, legs and shoulders.

"Looks like I blacked out, Veeni," Kedar looked at her and said.

"Blacked out?" Veena looked at him with trepidation. "Oh my God! That's why you did not open the door!"

Kedar did not say anything. Words would form on his lips, only to vanish without sound. He was gazing intently into Veena's eyes. "You are so careless about your health. Just look at the state you have brought yourself to," she was saying as her hand tenderly stroked his gaunt frame.

Kedar was still silent. "No wonder! I told myself that Bharaji has never uttered an angry word. Why did he speak like that today? On top of everything, look at this blazing heat. It's enough to make a perfectly healthy man feel restless and ill. And you had bolted the door from inside…" Veena continued, her words trailing off as a surge of emotion ran up from her heart to choke her voice.

Kedar was still gazing at her without uttering a word. Veena grasped his shoulders to shake him and remonstrated, "Bharaji, why are you staring at me like that? Why don't you say something?"

"What should I say, Veeni?" his lips parted to barely emit these words as he took her hand and placed it on his forehead.

"Why?" Veena exclaimed. "What do you mean by what should you say?"

"For God's sake, Veeni! Don't ask me anything," Kedar pleaded when she continued to implore him to speak.

"Don't ask you anything?" Veena rested his head on her knee and started to massage his forehead. "Look at the way you speak, Bharaji. Don't I have any right on you?"

"No."

"Why not?"

"Because I am a sinner."

"May your enemies be sinners! There is nobody who can compare with my brother," she said and moved Kedar's head into her lap.

"Veeni, I truly am a sinner."

"Leave it now, or I won't speak with you."

"Not just a sinner but a traitor too, Veena."

"Why don't you be quiet?"

"But you won't let me remain quiet either."

"If you are going to talk like this, you might as well not say anything."

"I did not suffer from any blackout, Veeni."

"You did not?"

"No."

"Then, you...?"

"It was an excuse – an absolutely false excuse."

"Why?"

"So that..."

"Tell me..."

Kedar was quiet.

"Why don't you speak now?"

"Veeni. It isn't something that can be told."

"Well! I am determined to ask."

Kedar was now absolutely quiet. His hands and feet were becoming cold and Veena was again vigorously massaging them even as she urged him to reveal his secrets. Finally, she warned, "You will see me dead if you don't tell me."

"Veeni, please don't ask. I beg of you."

"The more you speak like this, the more nervous I feel. Speak quickly, now."

"So you are bent upon asking?"

"Definitely."

"But I think you will start abhorring me."

Veena was perplexed. What could it be that will make me abhor him as soon as it comes out? Maybe he has committed some major crime. But even if he has murdered someone, could I still hate him?

"You can put that thought completely out of your mind," she asserted.

"Veeni," Kedar pulled himself together and said. "If this secret had been about me alone, I would have shared it with you without hesitation."

"So is it related to someone else too?"

"Yes."

"To whom?"

"To you."

As soon as he said this, Kedar lowered his eyes. Veena's hands, which were massaging Kedar's cold frame, paused for a moment before resuming their work. "Don't worry. Please carry on," Veena heard herself stutter.

"Veeni," Kedar said, his heart thumping in his chest. "I could not imagine that you would enter my life so quickly and rob my peace of mind in this fashion. I…I…" Every limb of Kedar's body reflected the words that he now uttered.

For a while, Veena's labours had managed to restore some warmth to them. But once again, they felt cold as ice.

Veena's eyes froze as she heard his words. Her gaze was transfixed on Kedar's face. Even after understanding what he had said, she was telling herself that maybe he means something else. Her hands, which were massaging his legs, withdrew themselves from his frame.

"What did you say?" A shiver of fear ran down Kedar's spine when he heard her query. But the conversation now had a momentum of its own and Kedar knew that he would not be able to rein it back until it reached its eventual destination. "Veeni! That is why I urged you not to ask. Since you forced me to speak and I am now ready to speak, I will not leave it incomplete. Veeni! You can look at it any way you like. Your love has brought me to a point where only two things can save me."

"What are those," the words pierced through her lips as she eased herself away from Kedar's body.

"Either my death or..."

"Or?" Veena asked worriedly.

"Or you, Veeni."

"What...What?" Veena got up from the bed. Kedar also sat up.

"Veeni," Kedar grasped her hand and pleaded, "If you want, you can save me."

Veena's heart was thumping. She wanted to leave the room and get away. Kedar pulled her hand to make her sit down again. Veena sat, not boldly like before but on the edge of the bed. She felt that Kedar was changing by the moment, turning into the form of some complete stranger. Seeing a

stranger in her home in the middle of the night sent all sorts
of signals through Veena's head.

"Speak up, Veeni," Kedar said. He repeated the phrase
several times but failed to get a reply from Veena. She could
not say anything even if she wanted to. She found Kedar's
words so extraordinary that she found it difficult to
comprehend that anyone could speak like that, let alone try
to find the words to respond to him. Giving in to Kedar's
insistence, she finally replied, "What is this that you are saying,
Bharaji? Do a sister and brother ever…" She could say no
more and got up from the bed.

"Veeni," Kedar's voice now had a note of urgency, "I
understand everything but …" He moved forward to grasp
her arm and again led her to sit on the side of the bed. "Veeni,
who says that we are brother and sister?"

"Our faith says so," Veena said, her eyes glistening with a
hint of anger.

"Sure," Kedar said with a show of confidence. "Sure, that's
what our faith says. But despite that, if I asked you to give
me the gift of life, would you decline? Your faith does not
ask you to dip your hands in someone's blood. Granted,
that I am a sinner and an immoral soul. But would the death
of this sinner allow your soul to be at peace? If you are ready
to bear that, so be it. I will be content with the thought that
my death has brought some happiness to Veena." Kedar
finished speaking and started to walk out of the house. He
had not yet reached the door that Veena followed him and
caught his arm. Kedar turned around to see a shower of tears
emerging from her eyes. Both sat on the bed again, not
speaking a word. Perhaps their ability to vocalise their thoughts
had momentarily deserted them.

Veena found her initial repugnance overtaken by a sense of profound sympathy for Kedar. She took the initiative and asked, "What do you want from me?"

"Haven't you understood yet?"

"No," Veena said even though she understood everything.

"Then, listen," Kedar said as he began to untie the knots that he had already loosened to let out the secrets that he held so close to his bosom. "Veeni, listen carefully. Stop looking at the ceiling and look at me. I have a great hunger for love. I received a lot of love from my mother but it could not stay with me for long. Thereafter, Beyji filled that void but the love that you have given me has changed the contours of my life completely. I get the feeling that the circulation of my blood and the rhythm of my breathing are both linked to your existence. In your absence, both would stop. I had made a firm decision that one day, I would ask your mother for your hand and I was confident that my proposal would not be turned down. But the walls of my patience crumbled when I learnt that you had already been promised to someone else. Despite a thousand attempts, I could not keep my emotions in check. Yesterday was like a day of reckoning for me. I really struggled with myself, tried my best to banish you from my system, but it seems that my efforts yielded the opposite results.

"Do you have any idea of my condition when you came in the afternoon? I was doing whatever I could to somehow forget you, and that is the reason that I spoke those terrible words, which I deeply regret.

"What brought me to you in the middle of this night? I don't know for sure but I believe that I was dragged here against my will. Veeni! I acknowledge my weakness. I also

know that at this time, when you are already betrothed to
someone else, I am guilty of breach of trust. Despite knowing
all that…" Kedar knelt at Veena's feet even before finishing
his sentence.

What was Veena's condition at this time? Repugnance
had been taken over by sympathy, which was now mingling
with pity. These were now combining to take the shape of
love. Feeling a surge of affection, she lifted Kedar from her
feet and got him to sit besides her, saying, "But you have to
think that something which is completely impossible cannot
be made possible by either you or me."

Sensing that he was close to success, Kedar grew bolder
and asked, "Do you refer to the fact that you are betrothed?"

"Yes."

"But we do not know yet if your in-laws will accept.
What if they decline Beyji's offer?"

"And what if they accept Beyji's offer?"

"In that condition, there would only be one alternative."

"What is that?"

"I had promised to bring the money by selling my house.
I will have to tell Beyji that I could not arrange the finances.
Without the money, there will be no wedding."

"Does it mean that you will deceive Beyji?" Veena asked
angrily.

"I wouldn't deceive her, Veeni. This would be for her
own good. The thousand rupees that she plans to waste on
your wedding would be saved."

"But do you realise that we will be unable to show our
face within our community?"

"That, Veeni, is mere talk. The community can do nothing to you. The community derives its pleasure out of the spectacle of lives being destroyed. Some people will gossip for a few days, then they will also become silent."

It was not clear if Veena liked Kedar's planning or not. But Kedar got worried when he saw the colour ebbing out of her face. Both remained silent for a while.

"Veeni?" Kedar asked more sternly. "Perhaps I am trying to force you. Does my proposal appeal to you?"

Veena gave no response.

"Veeni," Kedar kept his hand on her shoulder and said. "Are you angry over what I said?"

"No," Veena said without meeting his eyes.

"Then do you accept my proposal?"

Veena remained silent for a while, then nodded her head listlessly to signal her acquiescence.

That little movement of her head sent a wave of encouragement through Kedar. His joy was boundless, not taking any notice of the fact that her eyes were still showing their dejection.

"Veeni," Kedar pulled her closer and asked, "Can I say that from today, you are mine?"

Taking her silence as a sign of acceptance, Kedar put his arm around her neck and said, "Then why are you like this — as though you were upset?"

"Nothing. I am all right," Veena responded without looking at him. Kedar felt that he was playing with a lifeless puppet that had neither expression nor motion.

Suddenly, someone knocked at the door and called, "Veena, open the door."

"Beyji has returned," Veena said and ran to open the door. Kedar immediately lay down on the bed, feeling his heart sink again.

Mother and daughter were entering the room when Kedar heard Veena say, "Beyji! Bharaji has been in a bad shape today. He had blacked out."

Maya entered the room and showered her concern on Kedar. Upon learning that he was now feeling better, she said, "Thank God! May God look after you!" She started to massage Kedar and bombarded him with questions about his blackout – how it happened, when did it happen, etc.

Veena knew the question that Kedar wanted to pose to Maya before anything else. Pretending that she was going upstairs, she hid herself in the stairs and heard Kedar ask, "So tell us, Beyji. Did you accomplish your objective?" He received the response, "Yes. And very properly, too."

Veena did not deem it important to hear anything else. She went upstairs and made her mother's bed before lying down on her own.

After a while, she heard the door open. She leaned over the side of the terrace to look. Kedar had just left and was heading for his house.

CHAPTER 11

Somewhere in the distance, Kedar heard the morning siren of a factory. 'God! Is it already five o'clock? Does it mean that I did not sleep a wink the entire night?' he wondered. Scenes of the previous day's events, beginning with the time he had woken up in the morning till Maya's return late in the night started to unfold before his eyes. Soon, he found some of these scenes blending with others that had so far remained hidden under the cloak of the future.

'I hope she has been unsuccessful in her mission!' was the first thought to come to his mind when Maya returned the previous night. But his hopes collapsed like a house of cards when she began to speak about her achievement. Kedar saw the glow of pride and accomplishment in her face and found it impossible to stay any longer. Perhaps he wanted to retire to his solitude to contemplate his next step. Maya tried her best to persuade him to spend the remaining part of the night in her house but Kedar assured her that he was now fully recovered. Returning to his home, he went straight to his bed. He had little idea of how much time he spent that way, nor what thoughts went through his head. He felt as though his mind had separated itself from him and was wandering around on its own.

Dawn's cool breeze entered the room through the window and he felt himself momentarily drift into sleep as it comfortingly whisked the sweat away from his face. But he woke up with a start when he heard the sound of the siren.

His mind was once again drifting towards the same thoughts that he had already examined for hours and which always seemed to culminate in the same proposition: he should decline to pay the money. Veena would then be his forever. Although convinced of the success of this scheme, other thoughts cropped up before him. 'What if Veena's mother disapproves of this move? No doubt, she loves me like a mother. But how can I be sure that she would also accept me as a son-in-law? Not that she has very many options! And Veena herself can make her intent clear if she shows reluctance to go along with the current proposal. Anyway, we will cross that bridge when we come to it. The priority right now is for me to decide how I should convey my wishes to her. I should probably discuss this matter with Veena first. She will be coming soon for her lessons.'

He began to wait impatiently for Veena's arrival. The milky glow of dawn had broken through the night and was now spreading over the sky. He could see slivers of yellow sunlight trying to sneak into his room through the cracks between the doors.

Kedar got out of bed, quickly went through his morning rituals and changed his clothes. For several days now, he had neither applied oil to his hair nor combed them but he decided that he would today make up for the sloppiness of the previous days. He took out his razor to give himself a proper shave before turning his attention to polishing his shoes.

It was now past the time that Veena usually came and as he waited, he felt a familiar sense of despondency rising within him. His enthusiasm was waning rapidly.

Several dispiriting thoughts were adding to his sense of unease. 'Maybe Veena was offended by what I said? Maybe she has blurted everything to her mother.' He began a quick mental scan of scenes from the previous night, when he had revealed his innermost thoughts to Veena. He was trying to examine: 'Was there a frown on Veena's face after she heard my words? Was there any change in her demeanour? Did that comforting and affectionate expression start to evaporate from her face as I revealed my true feelings…?'

Kedar found it difficult to wait any longer. He felt his breath getting constricted as he decided to stay for a while in anticipation of the sound of the footsteps that his ears were straining to hear.

Why not go to Veena's house and see what's going on, he reasoned. But he wanted to have a word with Veena in private before encountering Maya. This requirement persuaded him to linger a bit longer in the hope that she might still turn up. His expectation unrealised, he eventually got up to go.

Before leaving his house, he once again combed his hair and buffed his already well-polished shoes. As he performed these chores, he was asking himself, 'Why is my heart pounding in this strange fashion, as though it wants to leave its moorings and wander all over the place?'

No sooner had he emerged from his house that he saw Vidya approaching him. She quickly clutched his hand and said, "Please come. Beyji has sent for you." Kedar felt the strength deserting his limbs as he heard her words. 'Perhaps Veena has narrated last night's incident to her mother! But was there anything in her manner to indicate that she might do so? Probably not! So why are they asking for me so early in the morning?' His mind was still preoccupied with these thoughts as Vidya pulled him to her home.

As he entered their house, Kedar saw that Veena was lying in the same room and in the same bed and Maya was sitting by her side with her finger on Veena's pulse. Kedar's heart sank.

"What happened, Beyji? What's wrong with Veena?" Kedar enquired as he quickly entered the room and grasped Veena's hand.

"I don't know," Maya replied. "She seemed fine when she went to sleep but was running high fever in the morning."

"Veena?" Kedar asked as he sat beside her on the bed. "How come you have this fever? You were fine when I left you last night!"

Veena gave no response and turned her face the other way when she saw Kedar. He also sensed that Veena could not bear the feel of his hand on her own. As Kedar sat on the bed, she slid away to the other side. Kedar's heart started beating faster.

"Don't worry," Maya said to Kedar as she got up from the bed. "It's the season for malaria. She will be fine after a bit of rest. Come, there are other things that I want to discuss with you." Kedar followed her into the porch where Maya brought into horizontal position a smallish charpoy that was inclined against the wall. Both sat on the charpoy.

"How are you feeling now?" Maya asked as she sat down. Kedar assured her that he was perfectly recovered.

"Beyji!" Kedar started the conversation quickly. "Why didn't you take the morning train? Would have saved you the trouble of returning so late last night."

Maya was glowing with satisfaction. She smiled and said, "The main purpose for which I had gone was accomplished soon and I saw no point in hanging around. Plus, I had left the kids behind."

"So how did the whole thing materialise? Kedar asked with a sinking heart.

"It was no great mystery. Turned out to be exactly what I had anticipated, in fact. Someone had blurted to them that we are in a state of complete destitution and that we would be handing over our girl to them without any dowry. They were spooked when they heard these rumours. The boy's mother! She is one who would steal a dead man's shroud. Initially, she was quiet. Then she started giving all sorts of excuses. She said that their boy was not ready for the marriage, that their finances were a bit tight. I understood what they really wanted. So I told her quite clearly that while there is nothing more precious than our offspring, our honour and dignity are even more sacred to us. I assured her not to worry about anything. Beg, borrow or steal, I would make sure that the wedding is done properly and their interests are looked after. So what if we are going through a difficult time now. We are aware of our standing and, god willing, we will ensure that our daughter is laden with gifts when she comes to your home."

"So what did they say?" Kedar asked as he tried hard to conceal the storms raging inside him with a false smile.

"Nothing!" Maya replied with rising enthusiasm. "She reacted as though she had lost her tongue. Then she replied, 'Fine, Sister. You have come especially for this purpose, so we can't let you down. We'll have to make our best effort to manage, one way or the other. We'll also work on persuading the boy. We have been getting offers from some of the best families but I don't have the heart to turn you down.' That deceitful hag! I could see clearly what she was getting at. She just wanted to make sure that we were in a position to meet her expectations. As for me, I heaved a sigh of relief when I heard her acceptance. What could I have done if she had made up her mind to decline? After all, you really can't put a price on your honour, can you? And it's all because you have a girl. If a boy's engagement breaks off even a dozen times, there's no problem. If one door is closed, a hundred others will be open. But for a girl, a broken engagement is no trivial matter. I really thank my stars that they have relented. There was precious little that I could do if they had not agreed. I would have been unable to show my face anywhere!"

Maya was speaking with great relish and Kedar frequently nodded in agreement but his thoughts were elsewhere. His mind was trying to come up with some grand scheme.

Kedar switched on when Maya stopped speaking but he had no idea where Maya had concluded her account. She remained silent for a long while, waiting for Kedar to say something. But seeing that not just his lips but also his eyes were motionless, she eventually asked, "Kedar! Where are you lost?" Before he could respond, Maya's own mind replied, 'What else would he be thinking about? Must be worried about how he is to accomplish this immense task. He's the one who has taken virtually the entire burden upon himself."

Kedar acted as though he had just awakened from a deep slumber. Leaving his train of thought midway, he replied, "This is really wonderful news."

Maya was desperate to hear Kedar say words to the effect that 'Beyji! Don't worry about anything...Everything will be fine.... I will soon arrange for the finances... etc.' Failing to receive the reassurance that she was looking for, she herself channelled conversation in that direction. "I believe that we could look at October or November for the wedding. The weather is nice by then, neither too hot nor too cold. Veena's mother-in -law was also saying that it would be good if we can get an auspicious date in November because by December the inauspicious stars rise and you won't get a good date for quite a while. If that happens, the wedding would surely be delayed by six months or a year. The sooner we are relieved of this burden, the better it would be. You never know who might try to hit you when you are down. Who's a friend and who's the enemy? One can never tell these days."

"I quite agree," Kedar said before falling silent once again. Maya was still waiting to hear something and said, "I feel that we should start working towards the arrangements right away. Every little bit adds up eventually."

"True! We will only get there if we start immediately. There are barely a couple of months to go," Kedar said feebly.

Maya was now beginning to feel concerned. She decided to take a more direct approach. "Well, it's all in your hands now. You had said…" Her voice trailed off as she asked herself if she had the right to put such pressure on him. Quickly changing the subject, she said "I suggest that you should send a letter today to Veena's father. You could also ask Sardarji to send word that he should return, if only for a couple of months. At the end of the day, he is the one who has to take charge. There are no secrets from you. We are going to accomplish this mission only if he comes back and makes serious efforts. He will also have to persuade Sardarji to assist."

Kedar realised that he was now neck deep in rapidly rising waters and being merely evasive would no longer work. Wrapping a string of rope hanging from the side of the bed around his finger, he said "I did bring up the matter with Sardarji yesterday, but…" His voice trailed off without being able to complete the sentence.

"Really?" Maya asked quickly. "What did he say?"

"He…He said…"His throat choked and he found himself unable to utter another word. Maya did not have to hear his words to understand the situation. The radiant glow that had suffused her face since the previous evening rapidly ebbed away. She found herself anxiously biting the index finger of her right hand.

"Then…Then its really…" Maya left her sentence half way. "Never mind. You write a letter today to Veena's Bhapaji. He will have to return and make some arrangements. If there is no other option, we might have to offer this house as collateral to borrow some money and tide over this problem. God willing, we will be able to repay the loan and get it freed again. But one way or the other, we have to manage the present situation."

Kedar lifted his head. He saw disappointment writ large on Maya's face as her eyes accused her. 'You are the one who promised,' she appeared to be saying without bringing the words to her lips.

Kedar found it difficult to stay there any longer. "I should go now. It's getting late," he said. As he got up, his eyes went once again in the direction of Veena's bed. It wasn't so far as to make their conversation inaudible to her. Kedar noticed that she still was still lying in the same posture, with her face turned the other way.

He put on his shoes and was about to leave the house when he heard a deep sigh emerge from the house. He paused for a second but was unable to decipher if the source was Veena or Maya.

He looked back inside as he left their house. Maya's head was drooping, propped up by her hand on the chin. Veena was now facing her, eyes seemingly transfixed on the door outside. She sensed Kedar's gaze falling upon her and quickly turned away again.

Kedar made his way through the bazaar. He felt that by the time he reached the shop, he would sprout a devil's horns on his head or somehow acquire an appearance so strange that neither his boss nor he himself nor anyone else would be able to recognise him.

Kedar felt like a man who had tried to leap across a crevice but was abruptly held back by the fear that he may fall inside if he is not able to cross the distance.

As he approached the shop, he felt that he had been completely transformed. Though the owner recognised him, he continued to feel that he would have difficulty in identifying his own image. He was wondering, 'Am I the same person that I was yesterday? Do I really have horns on my head, or are they just about to sprout?'

CHAPTER 12

*T*his was an unexpected and completely incomprehensible situation for the innocent young girl. She felt as though she had aged ten years during the course of the night. Until the previous evening, she was like any teenager, playful and light hearted like a butterfly, flitting around in her own little dream world. But the events of the previous night weighed her down to such an extent that Veena felt she was being crushed under her own burden.

She stayed awake through the night and by the time dawn broke, she was burning with a fever that was probably caused by her restlessness and lack of sleep.

Kedar came in the morning, and left after a while. Veena saw him but turned her face the other way. 'Why am I doing this?' she kept asking herself while he sat there. 'Because he is not the person that he was,' a voice inside her replied. 'But why?' she would query herself. And the reply would come, 'Because he is no longer like a brother; he wants to become something else.' When she thought of this 'something else', Veena felt that she had lost something very precious that she may never be able to find again. Her mind was alternating between two very different images – the first of a platonic friend, almost a brother, and the other…? Something new, nebulous and entirely different. The first image suffused her mind with a pleasing fragrance, while the second sent flames leaping through her heart.

Veena saw Kedar when he came that morning. When he held her wrist to check her pulse, she felt his touch. When he spoke, her ears heard his voice. But she felt strangely removed from the scene, as though watching a magician create an illusion – picking up a bit of gravel to transform it into a rupee coin and then turning it back into gravel. Every now and then, she thought she saw two images of Kedar instead of one – the *brother*, and the *other one* – the first a cup of nectar and the second, a poison chalice. Veena's soul was crying out, 'Kedar, my dear brother! What is this injustice that you have wrought? Alas! How I wish that I could always enjoy the brother's love.'

Although Veena's face was turned the other way, she could easily overhear the conversation between her mother and Kedar. She was hardly surprised by Kedar's response to Maya; indeed, she half expected him to decline point blank that he could not raise the money, though he had not yet done so in quite as many words. But Veena was sure that if not now, surely by evening Kedar would convey that 'Beyji, I'm afraid I have not been able to arrange any money at all.' And then? When he sees Beyji completely shattered by his comment, what would he do? Oh God! Brother Kedar…or….?

'And what if Bhapaji returns from Bombay and manages to arrange the necessary finances for the dowry and everything else – even if he has to mortgage this house? What would then be Kedar's fate? Will he really do as he threatened last night? Will he endure life without me? Or will the failure of his mission be such a shock that it will finish him off? Will that be the end of my brother Kedar? Oh God!'

Veena heard Kedar leave and turned on her side to glance at him. But he looked back at her just as he was leaving and Veena felt as if two arrows had emerged from his eyes and pierced her heart. She knew right away that this look was not from Brother Kedar but from the other one. And the realisation immediately made her look away.

As Kedar left, Veena's thoughts flew in every direction.

'Have I really started to hate him? No, not at all! Who says I hate him? But why did I get this feeling that I hate him when he looked at me? No, how can I hate him? ... Hate Kedar? ...Hate my brother?'

Veena felt dizzy, unable to think coherently. Maybe the fever was rising again. Everything looked a bit hazy, as though she was still dreaming about something. She asked herself again, 'Why didn't I talk to him? Why was I afraid of him? Is he a stranger? No, he is no stranger! Whatever he might be, he remains my Kedar – my brother Kedar!'

'And is that any way to treat a brother?'

'No. Not at all.'

'Why, then, did I act like this?'

'It was a mistake. A big mistake.'

'And can one apologise?'

'Certainly. In fact, do it today itself, when he returns from work. It would break his heart if you don't. He is such a sensitive soul, unable to tolerate even an angry word!'

'But what about the way he behaved that night?'

'That was cheap, if not downright immoral.'

'So?'

'So we'll see.'

Veena's mind played with these imaginary questions and answers for an interminable time. Buffeted by strong crosscurrents, her position was akin to a leaf caught in a raging storm.

By evening, Veena's fever had receded but she still felt weak and lifeless. Although wane, her face, however, looked more beautiful than ever, and made her eyes appear even larger than before.

Kedar did not come home for lunch that afternoon, nor did he show up in the evening. Veena was getting worried – afraid that he may not do something stupid. Maya was also getting concerned. Basant was sent to the shop to inquire, and returned with the news that he has gone somewhere for some urgent work.

The night went by, and Kedar had still not returned. A second day passed, and a third. Veena's heart was sinking, and anxiety was writ large on Maya's face too.

As the days went by, Veena's optimism was progressively waning, as were her patience and resolve. On the verge of tears, she asked herself, 'Oh! What have I done? Is it my behaviour that has taken his life?'

The fear that somehow she was responsible for his fate claimed Veena's appetite and sleep as its first casualties. Every now and then, her heart would cry out, 'Veena! Could his blood really be on your hands?'

It was now the fourth day after Kedar's departure. Until then, Veena had somehow managed to carry her burden. But this was now becoming impossible. Every pore in her body was crying out, 'Kedar! If only you were to come back safely this one time, I will cheerfully obey every wish of yours. I will do whatever you say. If I can give you more happiness as a wife than as a sister, I will do just that. But please come back safely just once, Kedar. Just one time!'

After tending to lunch on the fourth day, Maya sat beside Veena and said, "Veena! I think it would be best if you wrote to your Bhapaji. It is now four days since Kedar has not showed up. After all, how much claim can you exercise on someone else's son? No wonder they say that blood is thicker than water."

"But Beyji," Veena replied with sadness, "I don't even know Bhapaji's address."

"Oh! You are such an idiot!" Maya grumbled. "Couldn't you at least have noted his address?"

"I'll send Basant to the shop tomorrow and get it. But Beyji! Shouldn't we find out what has happened to Bharaji?"

Maya showed her annoyance at the question. Visibly irritated, she said, "Shouldn't *he* have informed us before leaving? But how can one complain about the behaviour of another's son? Let him do as he pleases. Anyway, make sure that you send Basant and get the address tomorrow morning. And write everything in detail."

Although she knew fully well what her mother wanted her to write, Veena inquired nevertheless, "What everything?"

"About your marriage, what else? Tell him that they have agreed to your marriage and want a wedding in November. He should come home as soon as he receives the letter. Alright?"

"I can't write this stuff," Veena said churlishly. "Marriage, marriage, marriage. The same subject every time."

"Don't act like a fool," Maya chided her. "You aren't a little girl any more. You are already in your sixteenth year. How much longer do you expect us to keep you in this house?"

Veena turned her face away. Maya was unable to read her eyes. Swept away by her own maternal instincts and the dreams of an incipient wedding, she was perhaps beyond deciphering the more complex aspects.

"Anyway, make sure you write," Maya said gently as she looked towards the door to see Kedar enter.

"Kedar?"

"Bhra..?"

Both words, one complete and the other partial, emanated simultaneously from mother and daughter.

Kedar had bent forward to respectfully touch Maya's feet. She lifted him up to embrace him and asked, "Where have you been all these days? Do you know how much we have waited for you?"

"Sardarji had sent me out for some urgent work," Kedar said and glanced at Veena, who felt her eyes lower involuntarily. Veena's arms, straining to rush out and embrace Kedar, remained dangling by her sides.

"Here! Please take these!" Kedar reached into his pocket and handed Maya eight one hundred rupee notes.

"This…this! Where did you get this, Kedar?" Maya asked, almost stammering with excitement.

"Sardarji gave it."

"Really? He's shown such magnanimity? Must say I did not have very high expectations from him."

"He's actually quite a noble soul, Beyji."

Thank God! May God shower His blessings on him for supporting unfortunate folks like us in our hour of need."

"So we should start preparations for the wedding, Beyji."

"Consider it done. This was just what we needed," she said. "Incidentally, did you write that letter to Veena's Bhapaji?"

"Yes, I did."

"And what did you write?"

"Whatever you asked me to."

"I hope you insisted that he should come immediately."

"I did."

"So what do you think? When will he return?"

"Let us see."

"Anyway, if you can accompany me to the market tomorrow? We could look at some fabric and some material for embroidery. Between Veena and I, we can start working on it. We can try to complete the major part now and get a tailor to stitch the clothes closer to the wedding. I also think there is no point in sending Veena to school any longer. How much can she learn in this month or two?"

"Fine. As you see fit," Kedar murmured politely and went off to his home to change. Maya tried to insist that he should wait to have some water or tea but he declined.

"Veena," she said after Kedar had left. "Make a glass of lemonade and take it to your brother. Poor chap! It's like a furnace out there."

Veena went off to the kitchen without saying a word.

$\mathcal{T}$he door was closed.

"Open it quickly or the lemonade will go bad."

"Okay!"

The door opened. When Kedar extended his hand to take the glass, Veena noticed that it was sickly yellow, like the hand of a corpse. She looked up and saw that his face and eyes were the same colour, or perhaps even worse.

Kedar emptied the glass at one go and returned to his bed to lie down.

"You haven't even changed your clothes," Veena sat beside him and said. At this point, she did not see Kedar as an outsider.

Not receiving a response, she gently stroked his forehead with her hand and asked, "I hope the lemonade wasn't tasteless today, like the tea the other day?"

"When?" Kedar lifted his eyes towards her and asked.

"The tea that you had the other day."

"That wasn't tasteless!"

"Did you drink it?"

"Yes. A whole cup."

"And was it sweet?"

"Must have been. Wouldn't have drunk it otherwise."

"Well! It wasn't."

"Maybe I didn't notice."

"Are you completely oblivious to these things? I was cursing myself that I had forgotten to add sugar...but why don't you talk properly?" Veena asked after a brief pause.

"But I am speaking," Kedar replied without looking at her.

Veena felt herself almost enjoying this little interlude, although Kedar's condition was also worrying her deeply. For a while, there was silence.

Veena was gradually trying to sit closer to Kedar, while he was shrinking away from her. The gentle caresses of Veena's hand on his forehead were like a piece of ice on his smouldering skin, ice that was so cold that it was burning him instead of cooling him down.

"Why aren't you looking towards me?" Veena placed his head on her knee and inquired. He moved away, and Veena again moved closer to him. He stood up, and Veena tugged his arm to again seat him beside her.

These simple gestures – seemingly innocent – were concealing a maze of complex equations that begged detailed questions and answers.

"Veena!" Kedar looked up at her once before lowering his eyes again and said. "Can't you forgive my mistake?"

"Me or you?" Veena put her arm around his neck and asked. "I've brought a lot of grief upon you."

"Not earlier, but you are certainly doing it now," Kedar grasped the fingers brushing his chest and said.

"Now?" she inquired nervously.

"Not once has that word escaped your lips today while addressing me."

"Which word?"

"Bharaji."

Veena felt a tremor go through her body. Tears welled in her eyes. She opened her mouth to say something but no words appeared. She could see Kedar's eyes overflowing with all the love that his heart could possibly pass into them. She saw her arms open involuntarily to embrace him.

Kedar did not say anything – nor did he move an inch. One hand was gently caressing Veena's back, while the other was resting on her head. Two or three warm droplets escaped his eyes and fell on Veena's dupatta. She used it to dab his eyes and soak the remaining moisture from them.

The arms loosened their hold.

"Veeni!"

"Yes."

"Won't you say it?"

Veena was quiet.

"Come on, Veeni! Call me 'Bharaji' once."

"….."

"Say it, Veeni! What are you trying to see in my eyes?"

"….."

"Aren't you my sister?"

"….."

"Veeni…Veeni!"

"….."

"Oh God! Say something quickly, Veeni...My heart..." and started pressing the left side of his chest with his right hand.

Tears were streaming down Veena's face. Her eyes were transfixed on Kedar's face, as though a magician had cast a hypnotic spell upon her. After Kedar had almost given up in his efforts to get her to speak, she said, "I'm afraid, Bhara..."

"Afraid of me?"

"No."

"So?"

"I... By marrying you..."

"Veeni, Veeni!" Kedar moved with the speed of light to cover her mouth with his hand. "Stop! Careful!" he warned sternly.

Veena's lips were trembling. Kedar's hand had quickly scattered the teardrops that had settled upon them.

"I... Was I born so that I would take *your* life?" Veena's sobs were echoing around the walls of the room.

"Veeni! What would people say if you were to be seen like this?"

"People can say what they like."

"Veeni! I wasn't serious. I am not going to die."

"No," Veena said in a voice choked with emotion. "You will have to fulfil your promise. And from where did you get that money? Tell me honestly!"

Kedar was quiet.

"You are ready to sacrifice your life. I know. I will fulfil your commitment. I will save you. I will be your wife..."

"Veeni!" Kedar covered her mouth once again and shouted. "Shut up! Say that word again and you will not see me alive. I will take my life before your eyes."

A pregnant silence again descended over the room.

"Come on, Veeni! My dear sister! Say 'Bharaji' once again," Kedar said and hugged her.

"Why don't you smile?" Kedar lifted her chin up and asked. "Come on, just once. My sweet sister."

Veena let out a forced smile.

"Go now, Veeni. May God preserve your marriage till eternity," Kedar said and withdrew his arms to his sides.

Veena had barely taken a few steps after leaving his room that she heard the door close and the bolt slam shut.

She paused at a hand pump along the road to wash her tearful eyes, perhaps to hide their secrets before she entered her own home.

Chapter 14

*N*otes of harmony were again returning to the musical strings in Veena's heart as they started to shed their recent discord. The turbulence that had engulfed her since that ill-fated night and left her feeing limp and listless was gradually receding and the grief that it had brought along was also ebbing away. The natural cheerfulness and sparkle of a young maiden were returning to Veena's countenance, though one particular source of anxiety continued to cast its ominous shadow over her.

Preparations for Veena's marriage were more or less complete, with just a handful of days remaining. As the wedding day approached closer, Veena's excitement mounted rapidly. The moment when her golden fantasies of entering the paradise of conjugal bliss would become reality, she reckoned, was about to arrive. But anxiety over Kedar's condition was also rising, as she saw a progressive deterioration in his health.

She was particularly distressed that she hardly got any opportunity to meet him because he would quickly find some excuse to slip away as soon as he saw her.

Veena would still visit his room, perhaps even more frequently than in the past. She wanted to quench Kedar's thirst for love as much as possible before leaving for her in-laws' home. But more often than not, she would return disappointed, with no option but to keep her feelings bottled up in her own heart.

When Kedar was not working, he tended to spend most of his time in his bed. He did not converse much with anyone. He gave the impression that he was looking for a place to hide whenever Veena entered his room. His predicament was aggravated by the fact that his desire to retreat from her was more than matched by her determination to come closer. Kedar found himself in a complete quandary, with no escape route in sight.

He remembered on one such day that Veena had a strong dislike for cigarettes and tobacco. In the course of one of their earlier conversations, she had mentioned that she would refuse to go to a cinema hall even when her Bhapaji asked her because of her aversion to the smell of cigarette smoke; she was convinced that she got a severe headache whenever she was exposed to it. So Kedar began to light up a cigarette whenever Veena stepped into his room, prompting her to make an early exit.

On more than one occasion, Veena snatched a cigarette out of his hands and threw it out of the room, even grabbed the pack of cigarettes from his pocket and flung it on the floor in anger. But it failed to have even the slightest impact on Kedar's habit. She swore that she would never speak with him again if he did not give up smoking, but to no avail. Some days, she would get agitated to the point that she would stomp out of his room and vow never to return if he continued with his addiction. But each time, she had to break her pledge even though she was seething with anger.

One evening, after many such episodes of getting angry and then making up, Veena's patience finally ran out. She entered Kedar's room and saw him lying in bed, swathed as usual in a bed sheet. Pulling the sheet with such force that it ripped down the middle, she said, "What's happening to you, Bharaji? You are always lying down in this despondent manner?"

Kedar sat up and stretched his arm to reach for one of the many matchboxes and packets of cigarettes littered on the table. Veena angrily grabbed his hand and said, "Why have you acquired this wretched habit?"

Kedar did not speak.

"Alright! Tell me what's happening to you, day after day?"

"To me? Nothing?"

"You are lying?"

"Not at all."

"How come you never laugh?"

"I do laugh."

"So laugh now!"

"There," Kedar said, managing a wan smile.

"No! Laugh out aloud!"

This time, Kedar laughed.

"No! Louder!"

Kedar cackled loudly – this time loud enough for the room to resonate with the sound.

"Yes! That's the way," Veena patted him on the back and said. "Promise that you'll always laugh like this."

"I promise."

"And also make another promise."

"What?"

"That you won't remain so stressed and downcast."

"Veeni!" Kedar let out a long sigh as he spoke. "Man cannot be in complete control of his destiny, can he?"

His words revealed such deep anguish that Veena did not consider it prudent to dwell on this topic any longer. "Any letter from Bhapaji yet?" she inquired.

"No," Kedar lowered his head as he spoke.

"How many days is it since you wrote to him?"

"Eight or ten days."

"Perhaps you should have written to him again."

"I will."

"Beyji is very worried. She says she is getting nightmares almost every day; hope everything is alright."

"Everything is fine, Veena. There is nothing to worry about." Kedar spoke these words boldly but in his eyes, Veena could see something else.

"What are you thinking about?" she gently tugged his shoulder and asked.

"Nothing."

"Why don't you tell me?" Veena's heart was thumping violently as she put the question. "So Bhapaji must have written. Tell me truthfully, Bharaji, is he alright?" she asked, shaking his shoulders.

"Veena! There was a letter. He cannot come yet."

"He can't come?" Veena stood up and asked, unable to remain seated. "But why?"

"He is not well."

"What?"

"Yes!"

"And why didn't you tell us? When did his letter come? What is the ailment?" Veena fired the questions in one breath.

"Its nothing dangerous. He is running fever."

"Fever?" Veena bit her finger and thought for a while before asking, "Where is his letter?"

"Its at the shop."

"When did it come?"

"Day before yesterday."

"And why didn't you tell us about it until now?"

"I… I thought… Beyji would get unduly worried."

Veena's face was turning pale. She could feel in her bones that something terrible was taking place.

Kedar hoped that the ground would swallow him. He cursed himself for his stupidity. Why did he have to blurt all this, he said to himself as he searched for a way to undo the effect of the words he had uttered.

"Veeni!" he steeled himself and said.

"Yes."

"Will you do as I say?"

"Tell me," Veena looked at his face, her eyes showing a blend of fear and suspicion.

"Promise me, Veeni."

"Promise what?"

"You will not tell Beyji about Bhapaji's illness yet."

"Why?"

"She has enough to worry about, what with all the arrangements for the marriage and all. She might just drop everything and collapse if she learns about this."

"Fine. I won't tell her." Veena said, feeling her throat dry up.

Veena persisted with many more questions about her father's welfare and somehow, Kedar managed to provide a satisfactory response to all her queries.

She left the room with a fresh worry on her mind, feeling her legs wobble.

CHAPTER 15

*W*edding day came quickly but there was still no sign of the person that everyone was waiting for. The neighbours were getting fairly vocal in their comments. 'What a shame! A daughter is getting married and the father is obsessed with making money! Couldn't he have managed to come just for a few days? Bombay isn't exactly across the seven seas!"

Kedar had scrounged around for every penny that he could muster, having exhausted all his resources. Every now and then, he would get annoyed with himself. 'What is this problem that I have invited upon myself for no rhyme or reason? What will happen now? Should I reveal the secret? But where would that leave me? I have called that lady my mother. Would she not begin to despise me from every fibre of her body? Instead of seeing me as a son, would she not curse me for being a snake hiding within her robes?"

But this was not the only worry gnawing at Kedar's innards. There was something else, even more dangerous, which was affecting not just his mind but also his entire body. The day that Veena would leave for her in-laws home was not far now. Kedar was aware of his relationship with Veena but found himself unable to fathom the thoughts going through his head. Like any brother, he was of course happy that his sister was getting married. Nor was he any less generous in his blessings that Veena should enjoy marital bliss to the fullest. His mind was untainted by any selfish thoughts. Yet, he was troubled – indeed, deeply anguished and in pitiable condition.

Often, he would try to probe himself to locate the source of his misery. He groped around in every corner of his heart, suspicious that there might still be some embers smouldering in some hidden cavity. But he did not find any. Then what is this ache – and why? What is this severe pain, which completely overwhelms him whenever it appears? Kedar simply could not decipher it.

How do you even *begin* to find a cure when you can't even find the ailment? The pain became more acute as the day of Veena's marriage approached closer. It grew to a point that Kedar could feel it arise with every breath he took, with every beat of his heart. It became especially severe with the mention of Veena's name, or even when her image flashed past his eyes, sending spasms through his entire frame. At such times, he wanted to fly away to some distant place where he could completely forget about Veena, to a world where the word 'Veena' simply did not exist.

Veena had still not shared Kedar's explanation of her father's illness with her mother. She spoke exactly as Kedar had coached her... 'There is enormous pressure of work...he will try his best, but might not be able to make it in time for the marriage...etc...' But she was deeply troubled by her father's reported illness and by her own grievance that he should have been present at her marriage. If this were all, she might have been able to prevent her cup of sorrow from overflowing. However, each time she looked at Kedar and empathised with his pain, she had forebodings of even worse tidings.

Veena wasn't so naïve that she could not comprehend Kedar's mental state. In some ways, in fact, she probably understood it better than Kedar himself, especially when she saw the manner in which Kedar was trying to evade her and the way he would close his door and retreat to his bed as soon as he came back from work.

Veena tried to do whatever she could to bolster Kedar's spirits. She would contrive situations – especially under the pretext of carrying a cup of tea for him – so that she could have a few private words with him. But Kedar simply refused to oblige. And when he saw that she was becoming a little too persistent in her efforts, he would feign irritation and say, "Veena! If you annoy me like this, I will leave this house and go somewhere else." Veena would return home unhappy and disappointed.

Veena could see quite clearly that Kedar was going through a major ordeal, as though willing himself towards some great penance or sacrifice. This was taking a visible toll on him and his health, his youth and his peace of mind were all getting completely ruined. But did Veena have any remedy for this condition? Perhaps she did have one, which she had thought would cure him and which she had tried to administer on him but for which he had signalled his refusal when he had prevented her from bringing the thought of a marriage with Kedar to her lips.

'Let me try once more. Maybe it would save Kedar's life!' The thought often crossed Veena's mind and kept cropping up even at this stage. Kedar did not, however, provide her the slightest opportunity to bring up the matter again.

The preliminary ceremonies for Veena's marriage, starting with her seclusion from strangers and the arrival of close friends and relatives got underway. The *halwai* came to prepare the wedding sweets, and the tailor arrived for the dresses. Groups of young girls started gathering to sing the wedding songs. Kedar was also compelled to take a few days off from work so that he could handle the arrangements. He immersed himself completely into the various chores, not permitting himself a single moment of leisure. He had perhaps discovered that his preoccupation with work dulled the sharp edges of his pain.

Veena had not seen Kedar for several days. For a bride to leave her seclusion and the intimate circle of women surrounding her in her room was inadvisable and would have been tantamount to a scandalous breach of conduct. She desperately wanted that Kedar should at least glance at her as he moved in and out of the house in connection with the wedding preparations. But her hopes remained unfulfilled. Kedar, it appeared, was making sure that his path would not cross her door.

The intensity of desire for an object grows with the realisation that it may completely elude one's grasp. Veena was by now desperate to meet Kedar at least once so that she could convince him about her eternal love and urge him to continue with his life. The longer she waited for the chance to meet him, the more fervent was her desire to arrange a meeting even though no opportunity was presenting itself. With just two days to go for the marriage and her desire to meet him still not satisfied, Veena was in a heightened state of anxiety.

She had been unusually restless that morning. Despite the best efforts of the girls and the imploring of her mother, she refused to eat. She spent the entire day thinking, 'Only this one day remains. Early morning tomorrow, I will be making my way to another home. Will I not be able to meet Kedar just once before I leave?'

Night fell. Members of the bride's marriage party started dispersing to different corners of the house to settle down for the night. But the girls were still beating the *dholaki* with full vigour. The singers' throats were becoming hoarse and the drummers' arms were getting tired but they showed no signs of bringing the revelries to an early halt. No sooner had one wedding song ended that a new one would begin.

A rug covering the floor of that small room accommodated almost fifteen girls sitting around the *dholaki* to sing their songs. Midnight gave way to one o'clock and the festivities still showed no sign of ebbing. It was, after all, the penultimate day! Only the remonstration of the elderly women, unable to sleep in the din, finally persuaded the girls to relent. Although some of the more energetic ones had come with the absolute determination to sing right through the night, the stern rebuke from the elders gave them no option but to reluctantly call it a day.

The six or seven girls who had come from amongst the neighbours went to their respective homes, while the rest spread around the room wherever they could find a place to sleep.

Surrounded by the girls, Veena lay in her bed contemplating her future through her mind's eye. The girls gradually drifted into a sound sleep but Veena was still awake. A lantern glimmered softly on the windowsill. One of the girls had turned the wick down before going to sleep. Veena's eyes were trying to focus on this flickering light. The room itself was completely dark, barring the pale glow around the lantern.

She must have been half asleep when she awoke with a start and sat up in her bed. She glanced quickly around the room at the slumbering figures. She then turned her attention towards Vidya who had been sleeping to her right and who was in the process of itching her thigh as she turned on her side, her sleep perhaps disturbed by a mosquito bite. Veena caught her hand and tugged at it several times until she opened her eyes to give her older sister a dazed look. Veena signalled her to get up and follow her as she herself picked up the lantern and quietly went out of the room. Vidya complied and tiptoed behind her. As they reached the stairs outside that led to the terrace, Veena whispered in her ear, "I will go upstairs to the rain shelter and wait. You go and call Bharaji."

As Vidya was leaving, Veena approached her and added, "Don't tell him that I sent you. Say that Beyji is calling him."

Veena made her way to the tiny rain shelter on the terrace where a tired old charpoy was resting against the side of the wall. She pulled it into a horizontal position and gingerly sat down. A little later, she heard the sound of approaching footsteps.

"Where's Beyji?" Kedar asked when he saw Veena and not her mother awaiting him in the rain shelter.

"It wasn't Beyji but I who sent for you. Please sit down for a while."

"But Vidya told me…"

"I am the one who told Vidya not to take my name. I knew that you would not have come if she had mentioned my name."

Kedar sat on the edge of the bed at some distance from Veena. He wanted to ask what on earth had prompted her to send for him at two in the morning but found himself unable to utter a word. The sight before his eyes had left him completely tongue-tied. Veena was wearing her crimson wedding dress and the strong colours of henna were glistening against the delicate skin of her hands in the dim glow of the lantern. The array of red bangles extending all the way up to her elbow would break into a gentle symphony each time she moved her arm. The ceremonial hairdo made her appear even taller than usual. Veena put out the lantern to make sure that nobody would see them.

"I hope you are not angry. I have disturbed your sleep at this late hour," Veena drilled her eyes into his ashen face and asked. Kedar wanted to say, 'Who the hell was sleeping anyway!' but words once again failed him.

"Won't you say anything, Bharaji?" Veena's face, her voice, her eyes were conveying just one emotion – the true colour of love – even stronger than the henna adorning her hands. The barrier of reticence that is erected by a maiden's inherent bashfulness had withstood the tides of her emotions for several days. But today's torrent of emotion swept away these defences in a flash. When Kedar continued to remain silent, she moved right beside him, held his hand in her own and pleaded, "Bharaji! At least say something now – I will be leaving soon." Her eyes filled up with tears. Kedar blinked his eyes, as though awoken out of a deep slumber by a splash of cold water, and said "What are you asking, Veeni?"

"Why are you angry with me?"

Kedar again fell silent. He had no answer to Veena's simple query but to respond, "Who says so, Veeni?"

"Come on, now! Please stop saying things just for the sake of it." Veena's pleading now showed an unexpected strain of toughness. "I'm not all that naïve!"

A look of intense seriousness had replaced the girlish innocence that characteristically marked Veena's face. Her words completely swept away the barricades of patience and restraint that Kedar had erected around himself, carrying his heart in their flow. Some unknown force wrenched out of him the words that he had vowed would never escape his lips as long as he lived. "Veeni! I cannot tell you. My sweet Veeni, please don't ask me to speak about this. I plead before you."

"I shouldn't ask? Knowing fully well that there is something in your heart? How can I not ask?" Veena moved near him, her face now very close to his. "You...you are drunk? Your breath..."

"Sure, Veeni. I did drink," Kedar interrupted her and said.

"But...Why?"

"So that I can get you out of my mind, and you can start despising me."

"Bharaji! What are you saying?"

"Nothing, Veeni! I'm sorry if I have said something that..." He started to walk out of the room even before he had finished his sentence but Veena caught his arm and forced him to sit down again. "What did you say? That I should *despise* you?" Veena tried to hold back a deep sigh but failed to prevent it from emitting quietly and merging into the silence enveloping the rain shelter.

"Yes, and that's also why I started to smoke. Go now, Veeni, I implore you. And don't ask any more questions, lest I have a change of heart. Please don't cry, my sweet Veeni. By showing your tears, you might..." Kedar's words choked in his throat. He freed his hand from Veena's grasp and retreated into a corner. Veena ran towards him and held him in her embrace. Her mouth opened to say something but perhaps the words crashed against her lips and turned back.

Kedar threw his arm around her and lovingly caressed her head, saying, "Veeni! May God protect your marriage! May a soothing breeze always blow in your direction! That is all that I ask for." He was trying to push Veena away from his body but she had clasped her arms around his arm so strongly that he was unable to break away. Veena was speechless but her tears were an eloquent expression of what her heart wanted to say.

"Your sobbing can be heard far away, Veeni. Please stop! For as long as I live, I'll live for you alone. I'll try my best to remain alive."

"I feel scared when I see your condition," Veena said, her voice heavy with grief.

"Scared?" Kedar said with a note of reassurance. "What should you be scared off, Veeni?"

Veena was unable to reply but deep inside, her heart was saying, 'I can see your footsteps taking you towards your death, Bharaji.' God alone knows if Kedar heard that voice or not. Maybe he did. Because if he had not heard it, why would he have said, "Veena, I will try to keep living."

"Bharaji!" Veena cried.

"Leave it now, dear Veeni. Your voice can be heard far away."

"No."

"Veeni! Leave me!"

Veena's arms slackened their grip and slid lifelessly by her side. She leaned her head against the wall of the rain shelter and began to cry. Still sobbing, she suddenly lifted her head - apparently impelled by some strong resolve — and said, "I take back the word that you made me utter the other day, when you made me say 'Bharaji'. I don't care about these bangles, or about the wedding finery. I...I want to spend..." Veena stopped in the middle of the sentence and glanced around her with bewilderment. A little voice inside her said, 'Silly girl, Veena! What are you saying, and to whom?' She now gave a closer look at the shadowy interior of the rain shelter but failed to spot Kedar anywhere. He had already left the place.

Veena's legs felt lifeless, as though they would be unable to take her down the staircase. Leaning against the wall for support, she slowly made her way down. She returned to lie down again at the bed that she had left a little while back. In the street below, a pair of dogs was wailing away in the night. Veena covered her ears to prevent this inauspicious sound from entering her ears but found herself unable to keep it out.

CHAPTER 16

Three days after Veena's marriage, Kedar returned to the shop. The door was still closed. He went up the narrow staircase to fetch the keys for the cash box.

When he reached upstairs, Attar Singh was stunned to see his appearance. The moment he set his eyes on Kedar, he asked, "What happened, Kedar? Have you been sick?"

"Yes sir," Kedar replied feebly. "I had fever."

"So you should have rested for another day or two," the proprietor said with unusual generosity. "You look really weak, as though you have been ill for months."

"No sir. I am absolutely fine now. May be just a touch feeble, but that should be alright in a couple of days."

"Well, as you wish," Attar Singh said as he handed him the bunch of keys. "A package of watches has come from Karachi and is lying at Central Bank. You can go some time during the day and bring it. I will be a little late today; a nasty belly-ache since yesterday."

"How much do we need to pay at the bank, sir?"

"Sixteen hundred. There is a bunch of hundred rupee notes in the little drawer in the lower part of the cash box. You can take that."

"Right sir," Kedar said as he went downstairs to open the shop doors and sweep the floor near the entrance.

A lot of work had piled up. Apart from bringing the accounts up to date, a number of watches and two or three clocks were also waiting to be repaired. He engrossed himself in the work. He planned to finish the bulk of pending work by evening and did not even take his break for lunch. But since it was important to go to the bank, he got up around 1.30 and took the money from the cash box. He went upstairs to ask the proprietor to mind the shop till he returned. Attar Singh, however, was feeling quite unwell and Kedar had to temporarily close the shop.

As he closed the doors and headed towards the bank, he saw Vidya and Basant approaching him.

"Bharaji!" Vidya exclaimed as she embraced him. "Where did you vanish?"

" I had to go for some work, Viddo," he said as he affectionately patted her head.

"Sister Veeni really misses you," Basant clutched his hand and said.

"She was asking about you right until her wedding carriage left," Vidya said in support of her brother. Kedar feigned disinterest in their comments and inquired, "Where were you two going?"

"We were coming to fetch you. Beyji is very upset," Vidya said in a serious tone.

"Alright! You go ahead. I'll finish the work at the bank and join you."

"No, no! Beyji insisted that we must bring you back with us."

"But Viddo, the bank will close!"

"Doesn't matter. I won't let you go. Beyji is crying."

"She's crying? Why?"

"I don't know. This fellow – a clerk or something; he's been sitting at home since a long time. Spoke quite rudely with Beyji."

"A clerk? Who is he?

"I don't know. He was threatening Beyji that he will declare us bankrupt and seize our home."

"Seize your home?" Mention of these words made Kedar set aside his work at the bank and without further debate, he accompanied the two kids to their house.

As he reached their home, he saw that Maya really was crying.

"What happened, Beyji?" Kedar removed the dupatta covering her eyes and inquired. "What's wrong?"

Maya's tears dried up when she saw him. Instead of responding to his query, she asked, "Where had you vanished?"

"I'll explain that later. First, you tell me who is the one who has been saying…"

Maya cleared her throat and started speaking, "What can I say, Kedar! No sooner do we deal with one calamity that we find another one hovering above us. Veena's Bhapaji never mentioned this to me."

"But what is the matter?"

"You know that money lender, Shamu Shah or whatever his name is. His clerk had come home today."

"What did he say?"

"He said that we have taken a loan from him."

"Loan? What for? Where is he?"

"He'll be coming back soon."

"How much was the loan amount according to him?"

"What he mentioned was no small amount. Two and a half thousand."

"Two and a half thousand!" Kedar felt the blood drain from his body.

They had just started talking when a diminutive, sharp looking fellow entered clutching a large accounts ledger under his armpit. Maya gestured with her eyes that he was the one.

"Come, Lalaji! What is the matter?" Kedar looked at him apprehensively and asked.

"Is he the one you were waiting for?" Instead of responding to Kedar, the stranger looked at Maya and asked. After receiving the whispered affirmative from Maya, he turned towards Kedar and said, "Sir, you are a man of the world. You would understand that doing business and showing compassion are two very different things. Mr. Panna Lal's association with our establishment is not new. We've had a cordial relationship that goes back at least ten or twelve years. He is an honourable man and his word is as good as gold.

"But, Sir, you are wise and I am sure you know perfectly well, bad times can fall on anyone. Fate does not even spare the kings and queens. Otherwise, this amount of two or two and a half thousand would have been no great issue. Believe it or not, thousands of rupees have been taken and returned by your husband without a soul getting to know about it. But eventually, his luck ran out. Business truly is a game of chance. If the dice rolls your way, you're made. If not, you are nothing.

"Now, our boss has known Mr. Panna Lal for a long time. For small amounts like these, we did not even bother to enter the transaction into the ledger. He would take a loan and return it at the appointed time. But since his business came to a halt, this amount has remained outstanding. Not that we are excessively worried. We know that this is not a big sum for a reputed family. Still, when the due date for repayment of the principal comes, we have to take some action, don't we?"

Kedar started to get the picture as the clerk spoke – recognising his last comment that 'we have to take some action, don't we?' as an implicit threat of legal proceedings.

Following up on his preamble, the clerk opened the voluminous ledger and began to read out details of the account – principal as well as the interest overdue – adding to twenty five hundred and twelve rupees. Panna Lal's signature at the bottom of the page precluded any possibility of discussion or debate on the issue.

"You didn't know anything about this, Beyji?" Kedar asked with growing concern. She replied, "He never even mentioned this to me. He would always tell me every little detail, be it work-related or personal. But not once did he make any reference to this."

"Alright, Lalaji," Kedar addressed the clerk gently. "Allow us to send him a letter to confirm this. In five or six days, we should get a reply from Bombay. Thereafter, as you…"

"Come now, sir," the clerk interjected. "The wise man says that he would prefer the miser who responds promptly over the bountiful one who is late. The amount is now almost due. Barely three days are left, and after that its time! If there is even a penny's difference in accounts, the transaction can remain outstanding for a hundred years. Besides, if you are going to raise the issue of accommodation or leniency, let me say that it will come to naught."

"But Lalaji, at least we have to confirm with him. Even if your accounts are absolutely in order, there is no harm in reassuring ourselves."

"You can reassure yourself to your heart's content. Look here! Panna Lal's own signature! You can of course reassure yourself as much as you like. But please don't mind if the day after the amount comes due, a lawsuit gets filed. It could unnecessarily cost you another two hundred rupees or so. Doesn't do *me* any harm!"

There was now a touch of sharpness, even arrogance in the clerk's tone.

Kedar was in deep thought. Maya felt her heart sinking. After thinking for a while, Kedar spoke, "Alright. Why don't you renew the loan? That way there is no danger that there will be a default on the payment."

"Lalaji, why do you speak the words of an innocent child? I really don't know how I should respond when you speak like this," the clerk sneered with more than a hint of contempt.

"What do you mean?"

"I mean that if people like us start renewing the amount without receiving any payment, how are we expected to run our business? Besides, I am sure you appreciate that one will scatter seed only where he hopes to get a crop. Only an idiot would waste it when he knows that the land is infertile. Earlier, things were different. Panna Lal had a running business and we knew that we could scoop a pan or two from the flowing stream. But now, he is himself employed at a meagre salary, facing God knows what kind of difficulties in distant lands! I hope you would pardon my expression but if something were to happen to the lady of the house or if she chooses to pack up and go away, we would be left high and dry, wouldn't we?"

Kedar could see that the clerk was a tough nut to crack. He was clearly more worried about the prospect of losing the entire amount than he was about its prompt repayment. That was, perhaps, the main reason that he had timed his visit just as the amount was falling due for payment.

"So what do you want us to do?" Kedar inquired. Maya appeared in a state of absolute shock over this latest calamity.

"Lalaji," the clerk said sternly. "You can listen from one ear or the other. There are no halfway measures available now. Whether you do it with ease or with difficulty, the amount will have to be repaid. Or else…"

"Or else what?"

"The matter would have to go before a court."

"So you would stoop to that level? You would be willing to drag into a court and bring disrepute to the wife of the man with whom you have enjoyed close dealings over the years, the man from whom you have earned thousands of rupees?" Kedar's words were laced with anger.

"No need to get excited, Lalaji," the clerk said condescendingly. "This is not a matter of repute or disrepute. It is just a question of business. Besides, you are a man of the world. I'm sure you understand the situation. Everything revolves around money. When people like us lend thousands of rupees without asking a question, we are not doing any favours to the recipient. Nor do we think that the recipient is engaging in an act of great nobility when he pays us back. When you have a running business, there is always flexibility in accommodating your problem. But there is no room for flexibility when the business comes to a standstill. Who extends concessions to anyone, Lalaji? Concessions are only available to running concerns. Everything flows in the direction of the current. As soon as the business stream runs dry, all concessions disappear."

Kedar was seething with anger as he heard the clerk's cold and insensitive discourse, feeling as though his own dignity and self-respect had been assaulted. He was unwilling to put up with such insulting behaviour, especially in the presence of Maya who was like a mother for him. He felt that he could no longer tolerate the clerk's callous words, nor indeed his company in the room. Moreover, he had seen that his pleas had fallen on deaf ears and there was nothing further to be gained through this approach. Summoning all his dignity, Kedar replied, "If you are so distrustful, you can take half the amount now and prepare fresh documents for the remainder."

Hearing Kedar's words, the clerk realised that his gambit had paid off and this was the time to try to convert that 'half amount' into the full amount. Meanwhile, a shiver ran down Maya's spine as she heard Kedar's promise. She knew that after Veena's marriage, they were penniless; indeed, there were several small bills that still had to be settled. Afraid that there was no way of paying even half the amount, she hoped that the clerk would turn down Kedar's proposition. Her house was her only remaining asset and she dreaded the thought that she might have to sell it to somehow square the accounts.

"Come on now, Lalaji! What difference would it make to you if it were the entire amount or just half the amount? If you are going to make the effort to raise half the amount, you might as well go the full distance and finish the matter off," the clerk said.

Kedar responded by reluctantly offering to pay fifteen hundred rupees up front, with fresh papers to be drawn up for the remaining one thousand rupees. But seeing his prey collapse, the clerk was going for the jugular. After much unpleasantness and acrimony, they finally agreed that Kedar would pay fifteen hundred rupees immediately and the house would be mortgaged with the lender for the remaining one thousand rupees with the further understanding that this amount would be settled within two years.

Kedar accordingly took the fifteen hundred rupees out of his pocket and handed the money to the clerk. The clerk's ledger was duly corrected to reflect the payment into the account. The house, fortunately, was registered in Maya's name and it was agreed that preparation of the mortgage papers would be a fairly straightforward task. The clerk was impatient, and Kedar too was anxious to complete the formalities quickly. Having relieved his master of fifteen hundred rupees, he felt that he must leave the scene at the earliest.

The court papers for the mortgage were obtained and a public notary was requested to come to the residence to complete the papers without delay. Kedar signed the documents as one of the witnesses and a neighbour was asked to sign as the second witness. That left one remaining formality – to get the papers attested at the court. It was agreed that

Maya would go to the court the following morning to get this done.

Promising to return the next day, the clerk tucked his register under his arm and left. Kedar, meanwhile, completed yet another important piece of work. He wrote a letter in his master's name and after making sure that Maya was not paying attention, took Basant aside and handed him the letter and bunch of keys for the shop. "Here, son! Take these to Sardarji's shop. Open the door and take the stairs upstairs to his home. And don't give him any details about yourself or about me," he told the youngster.

Maya, meanwhile, had been a passive spectator to the proceedings. Like a sleepwalker enacting a dream, she complied with Kedar's instructions without being aware of what exactly was going on.

CHAPTER 17

$\mathscr{V}$eena had gone to her in-laws place. The marriage had been a bustling, cheerful affair. Maya had been generous in her allocation of gifts and dowry and while she may not have been able to exceed the expectations of the boy's family, they were by no means disappointed. With the daughter's marriage, a major burden had lifted off her shoulders. She had just begun to heave a sigh of relief when a new crisis descended upon her, one about which she had no inkling whatsoever.

Kedar turned up at the nick of time and helped in averting what looked like a certain catastrophe for the family. All that remained was for her to go to the court the following morning and get the documents attested. She had already been deeply indebted to Kedar. Without the eight hundred rupees that he had placed in her palm, the marriage would have been well nigh impossible. And on top of that, he had now performed this second miracle by providing a full fifteen hundred rupees. How could she ever repay his kindness? Blessings for his well being emanated from every pore in her body.

Nevertheless, Maya did nurse one major grievance against Kedar – his disappearance at the time of the wedding. He had simply vanished without informing anyone about his whereabouts. And that too at a time when her husband was not around and she was really dependent upon Kedar for everything. It was a matter of great regret that for two entire

days and nights, he was nowhere to be seen. What made
things even worse was that poor Veena continued to wait
for him right until her carriage left their home after the
wedding.

Maya tried to ask Kedar about the fifteen hundred rupees
that he had given to the clerk but he refused to answer. And
when he swore her to silence to prevent her from inquiring
further into the matter, she couldn't help thinking, 'What if
this money belongs to the shop? What will he tell the master
if the cash was given to him for a specific purpose?' But
Kedar's oath of silence was like an iron barrier that she could
not cross. After the clerk left with the cash, Kedar looked
distinctly uncomfortable as he came inside the house. She
asked him to sit beside her and asked, "Kedar! So tell me
now where had you vanished the last couple of days?"

Kedar gave no response as Maya continued, "Really! At
least you should have thought of Veena, who cared so much
for you. She was pining to see you just one last time right
until the departure of her *doli* (bridal palanquin). How could
you act this way?"

Kedar moistened his dry lips with his tongue and said,
"What can I say, Beyji? It was due to the nature of the work
that I had to do."

"The hell with such work! The poor girl was wailing
inconsolably and you were only concerned about your work?
Ask Viddo or Basant and they'll tell you how she passed
those two nights. Every few minutes, she would ask me,
'Beyji! Why don't you send Basant to fetch Bharaji?' A little
later, she would make the same plea to Viddo. The poor
kids ran off their legs going back and forth. But who knows
where Kedar sahib had disappeared," Maya said as she reached

for the shelf and handed Kedar a small photograph, no more than half the size of a post card. "Here! She asked me to give it to you as a token of remembrance."

Kedar accepted the photograph. It showed a young girl of eleven or twelve, with red ribbons around her two pigtails. She looked an absolute doll.

Kedar's hands trembled as he held the picture. His eyes filled up with tears of remorse. He was repenting his folly and his heart was cursing him, "Villain! Such cruelty! How much you have hurt that innocent girl! Why couldn't you have met her just one time before she left?"

"Beyji…" Kedar started as though he wanted to change the subject. "My health is deteriorating by the day."

"That's perfectly obvious. I've told you so many times to consult a decent doctor. But you just keep putting it off."

"I have consulted a doctor."

"So what did he say?"

"He said that the climate here does not suit me."

"Climate does not suit you?"

"No."

"And so?"

"The doctor says I need a change of climate, that I should go to the hills for a while."

Maya pondered the implication of Kedar's comments. He had become such an inseparable part of their family that it was hard to see him absent even for a day. Seeing the anxiety on her face, Kedar said, "Please don't worry, Beyji. Think that I am besides you. I promise to return fairly soon."

Maya heaved a deep sigh.

"In fact, I am planning to leave by tomorrow itself."

"That soon? Let Veena come back. She will be here for her post-wedding visit in two or three days at the most."

"Its not advisable to wait that long, Beyji. The doctor had told me to leave right away. He said that my life is in danger."

His last sentence came like a seismic shock to Maya. Feeling gooseflesh all over her body, she looked worriedly at Kedar and whispered, "Is that right? Then go, by all means. I won't come in your way." Maya's heart was in her mouth. Suppressing the surge of motherly emotion that was rising through her, she inquired, "Which way are you planning to travel?"

"Somewhere close by...Maybe to Muree."

"And for your expenses?"

"I'll be able to arrange that," Kedar said as he glanced at the ring in his little finger, which had been given to him as a gift by his master during the previous month.

"You'll go without meeting Veeni? She'll die when she learns about this."

"I'll try to meet her on my way. Gujarkhan isn't all that far from here."

They were still chatting when someone knocked at the door and called.

Kedar got up immediately as he recognised his master's voice. Moving towards the stairs at the rear of the house, he whispered into Maya's ear, "Beyji, its Sardarji! Please don't tell him anything about me. Just tell him that Kedar has not come here since yesterday. Swear upon me that you won't tell him anything." And he ran up the stairs to the rooftop.

"Do come inside," Maya said as she opened the door. A bulky body entered the room and parked itself on the bed.

"Are you from Panna Lal's family?" Attar Singh fired his first question at Maya.

Maya lowered the dupatta over her face and said, "Yes sir. I hope you are well. How is the Sardarni?" Maya's heart was thumping. She was embarrassed that the Sardar must think quite poorly of her. She had not even gone to his house to express her gratitude for his noble gesture in providing timely assistance at the time of the marriage. She was also anxious to get the latest information about her husband, but the Sardar touched upon a very different subject.

"Everything is fine," he replied perfunctorily as he gave a disinterested look around the room. "I had come to inquire Kedar Nath's address. I learnt from the bazaar that he lives in a house near to yours. Since his door was locked, I thought I would ask you. May be you would know!"

"We have not seen him since the day before yesterday," Maya said even though she felt her throat choking over the lie. 'What would I do if Kedar starts to cough, as he often does, or if he somehow suspects that Kedar has gone upstairs,' she thought.

"Really!" Attar Singh said, unable to conceal his disappointment. "Do you know of any other place that he visits frequently? I have some very pressing business with him."

"I am afraid I don't know of any other place that he frequents."

"Alright," Attar Singh said, his face going visibly pale. He was going to get up to leave when Maya beseeched him with folded hands, "Sir! If you could stay for just a few minutes? I wanted to ask about a couple of things."

"Go ahead," he sat down again and said. He had not forgotten about the injustice he had done to Panna Lal six months ago, or the fact that he had not seen Panna Lal's face thereafter. "So tell me, where does Panna Lal work these days... Is he here or somewhere out of town?"

His question struck Maya like a bolt from the blue. Eyes transfixed on his face, she pondered over his words. This was precisely the matter that she had wanted to inquire about. Could it be that he was talking about someone else? Or was he simply trying to conceal his generosity at the time of the wedding? "Sir! In fact, I had myself wanted to ask you about him," she said.

"Ask me?" Attar Singh responded with a puzzled look. "I don't know anything about him."

"Sir, you are the one who has sent him to Bombay. I've been meaning to come to you to find out about his programme but preoccupation with the girl's marriage kept me from coming. It is not good to flatter someone in his presence but to be honest, Sir, we acknowledge our gratitude to you with every breath we take. By giving us eight hundred rupees at a crucial time, you truly became our family's saviour. Very few have such a big heart. May God shower His blessings upon you."

Maya's words fell on Attar Singh's ears like some foreign language that he could hear but was unable to comprehend a single word. Finding himself at a complete loss of words, he paused for a long time after Maya had finished speaking.

"Bibiji! Who are you talking about? Perhaps you have not recognised me," he finally said.

Adjusting her dupatta around her face, Maya spoke softly, "Sir, how can we not recognise you? You have provided us our livelihood for the last six years. There are some who will do you a favour and remind you of it a thousand times. And then there are those like yourself who actually try to hide your acts of generosity. Truly, it is people like you who are holding up this earth."

"But Bibiji, I have done nothing for you. It is now five or six months since your husband left my employment."

Maya's head was in a tizzy. She still thought that Attar Singh was reflecting typical nobility and magnanimity and that she was somehow unable to comprehend him. She said, "Sir, when do you think he will return? It's almost six months now. He couldn't even come for his daughter's wedding. He did write that he would come back whenever Sardarji permits – that there is heavy pressure of work at present. Of course, he can stay as long as you think is necessary. And his salary does come home at the start of every month. What more can we ask for? Except that there are these small kids who are dying to see him soon. It would be wonderful if he can be given leave for a few days. At least the kids will be able to meet him."

By now, Attar Singh was completely mystified. He felt that his efforts to understand this matter were only dragging him ever deeper into the quicksand of this enigma. Reflecting his growing annoyance with the whole affair, he said impatiently, "Bibi! I fail to comprehend your words. Who sent him to Bombay? Who gave you money for the girl's marriage? I have neither a shop nor any agency in Bombay.

That's why I am emphasising that you must be making some mistake. Your husband must be working with someone else now. It's been quite a while since he left my employment." Finishing his sentences in a rush, he indicated that he was ready to leave and got up from the bed.

Attar Singh's words left Maya's mouth ajar in amazement. She knew that if she contradicted him again, he could well take it as a sign of stubbornness bordering on disrespect. His own growing irritation and surprise suggested that he could not be lying. She felt her head spinning but persisted with her inquiry because she wanted to arrive at some conclusion. With this objective in mind, she asked, "Does Kedar work with you?"

"Yes, he does."

"And you didn't transfer him from agency work to look after the shop until my husband returns from Bombay?"

"I certainly employed Kedar in place of Panna Lal but I had fired Panna Lal on the same day that I had hired Kedar for the job. He himself handed over charge of the shop to Kedar and collected his salary before leaving. I have no idea where Panna Lal went thereafter. Indeed, had I known anything, why would I have bothered to inquire about him as soon as I entered your house?"

"And you don't know anything about him?" Maya's eyes were locked on his face and she appeared to be in a barely conscious state as her lips uttered these sounds. For a fleeting moment, she wanted to call Kedar from upstairs so that the whole matter could be clarified in his presence. But she felt herself constrained by her vow to Kedar.

"But Bibi," Attar Singh saw Maya's distressed state and spoke more gently. "Who told you that I had sent Panna Lal to Bombay?"

"It was Kedar."

"Kedar?" Attar Singh paused for a while before asking; "About the salary that you say you receive every month... does that come to you through a money order?"

"No, Sir. Kedar brings it home to me. He says that Sardarji himself gave it for me."

"Very strange! I have never given him a penny for this purpose. Nor was there any reason to give, since Panna Lal no longer works for me."

Attar Singh reflected on this for a long while and said, "Bibi! You also mentioned that I had given something for your daughter's wedding?"

"Yes, Sir. Kedar gave me eight hundred rupees and said that he had received them from you. Did you not give that money?"

"Not at all. I did not even know that your daughter is to be married."

"Sir, the marriage, mercifully, has already taken place. The *doli* left the day before yesterday."

"I see! Did Panna Lal ever write to you during this period?"

"Sir, there were several letters from him. The last one, in fact, arrived only a few days before the wedding."

"Really? Could I see any of his letters?"

"Well! All the other letters came to Kedar. He would read them out to me and then keep them. But the postman gave this last letter to our younger son. Kedar was not home that day." Maya stood up to look for the letter, found it in a corner and passed it to Attar Singh.

After a mere glance at the postcard, Attar Singh exclaimed, "But this is clearly Kedar's handwriting. I know the writing of both pretty well." He turned the postcard around to look closely at the post office stamp and pronounced, "Despite a clear attempt to erase the stamp, it is evident that this has come from a Rawalpindi post office and has been posted to Kedar's address."

Attar Singh again retreated into deep contemplation. Suddenly lifting his head up, he asked, "Tell me, Bibi! Did Kedar also give you a certain sum of money today?"

Maya froze in shock. Her lips were on the verge of saying 'yes' when she heard the syllable 'no' emerging instead. She did not take long to figure out that Kedar had probably brought the money from the shop and by acknowledging that she had received the money, she might bring major troubles upon him.

Attar Singh found it difficult to linger any longer in her house. Maya had many more unanswered questions but he abruptly got up and left. Maya immediately ran upstairs to fetch Kedar but there was no sign of him.

ware that Kedar had taken unduly long to finish the work at the bank, Attar Singh was getting increasingly impatient. However, he wasn't yet ready to start doubting the intentions of someone as sincere and hardworking as Kedar.

The clock struck four, and he was still waiting. By five o'clock, there was still no sign of Kedar and Attar Singh's annoyance was turning into a real sense of unease. Although his upset stomach was still bothering him, he had no option but to hire a *tonga* and visit the bank to ascertain the position. He felt the ground slip beneath his feet when he learnt that Kedar had not come to the bank at all. 'Perhaps he has made off with the sixteen hundred rupees,' he thought. He toyed with the idea of going to the police station to file a report but then changed his mind and asked the *tonga* to head for the shop instead.

The doors at the shop were still shut. His heart by now was thumping against his chest and he was on the verge of asking the *tonga* to take him to the police station when he heard his little girl call him. He went upstairs into his home and learnt that a young boy had delivered a letter and the bunch of keys for the shop.

Attar Singh hurriedly opened the letter and started to read. It said,

"My provider!

"You must be concerned over my delay in returning. Allow me to say that there is no reason to be worried. Circumstances have taken such a strange turn that they have prevented me from coming back. Please do not think that I am ungrateful; as long as I live, I will remain indebted for all you have done for me. I had virtually nowhere to go when you not only provided me employment but also trusted me to the extent of leaving your entire business in my custody. How can I ever forget that?

"With what face should I come before you and acknowledge that instead of depositing your sixteen hundred rupees in the bank, I have spent them elsewhere? Where did I spend them and why? I cannot answer this at present, except to say that by using the money in this manner, I have neither acted dishonestly nor committed a sin. I had to spend the money for the sake of a person whose reputation and honour were in peril.

"If you feel that for committing this offence, I should be prosecuted in a court of law, I will promptly present myself in the court and acknowledge my crime without attempting to offer any defence and I will consider it my moral responsibility to cheerfully accept whatever punishment is decreed. However, if you were to act magnanimously and not move any legal proceedings against me, I assure you that I will return every penny that I have taken. I have confidence in my earning capacity and I am sure that it will not take me too long to pay back this amount.

"I am sorry that I cannot face you until I have paid back your money. I hope that in the meanwhile, you will be able to find someone else who can manage the shop. If I am still alive after I have paid back your money, and if you have deemed it appropriate to forgive me, I sincerely hope that I will be able to come under your protective shade once again. But under the present circumstances, it appears that I will be unable to stay here. It is not just the money that is forcing me to leave this place; there is also another pressing reason that prevents me from staying here at this time.

"May I hope that you would understand my feelings in the same manner that I have submitted them before you? I would then consider myself to be privileged despite my misfortunes.

"In your service for ever

Kedar"

Attar Singh read the letter and found himself getting sucked into an ever-deepening whirlpool of bewildered thoughts. He finally called the *tonga* that was still awaiting him in the street below, said that he had decided against going to the police station and sent his son down to pay the fare.

He then went downstairs and opened the shop. Going straight to the cash box, he lifted the top to check its contents. Apart from the sixteen hundred rupees, it contained a fairly large sum of cash and some gold and jewellery as well. Everything was as it should have been – not a penny more or less.

Kedar's letter had a strange effect upon him and much of his anxiety evaporated. His main concern now was to somehow try and stop Kedar from leaving. He believed every word of the letter because over the last six months, he had acquired a fairly good idea of his character. He also accepted that for someone as talented and industrious as Kedar, it was not difficult to repay this amount. His major worry at this point, indeed, was the potential absence of Kedar. Considering the manner in which Kedar had not only assumed responsibility for running his shop but also added significantly to his income by carrying out the repair of watches, his departure would be an enormous blow to Attar Singh's business. He also knew that it was by sheer good fortune that he had found someone like Kedar to work for him and he was afraid that losing someone like that was surely a sign of further misfortune lurking around the corner. He decided that he must do everything possible to find Kedar so that he could prevent him from leaving and also assure him that he was not upset over the misappropriation of the money.

He knew the street in which Kedar lived and after closing the shop, he set off in that direction.

We have already read in the previous chapter about Attar Singh's visit to Panna Lal's house, what he learnt about Kedar when he went there and the deep anxiety with which he left the place.

After leaving their house, Attar Singh persisted in his efforts to locate Kedar. He went wherever he thought he might find him and even scanned the railway station but to no avail.

$\mathcal{M}$aya was unable to sleep that night as she tried in vain to grapple with the intricacies of the puzzle. She found her situation akin to a traveller who is about to be devoured by a lion as he is passing through a forest but to his good fortune, some invisible hand plucks him out of the forest, only to deposit him amidst the raging torrents of a river.

Several times that night she got up and went to Kedar's house, only to return disappointed after finding the door locked. More than once, she woke up with teeth clenched in anger, asking, 'Why did he keep me in the dark all this while? What was his purpose in doing all this? Why did he have to weave such a complicated web? Would an honest man delude others in this manner?' But then her thoughts would turn to the selfless and caring way in which he had treated her family and she would start to repent her accusations. She would, instead, ponder: 'How would I have managed without Kedar's helping hand during this critical period? How would I have married my daughter, or run the expenses of this household, or removed the burden of debt from my shoulders?'

All these thoughts, however, scattered like autumn leaves in a storm when her mind turned towards her husband. With a sobbing heart, she thought, 'If the Sardar described everything truthfully, it means that my husband must have set off somewhere when he lost his job on the day that he had set out to borrow money from the Sardar for Veena's marriage.

But where could he have gone? And what if he did something stupid when he was in a state of depression? Didn't he often speak in inauspicious terms?' By this point, Maya's strength and courage would wane and she would bury her face in her pillow and sob uncontrollably.

Somehow, oscillating between confusion over Kedar's behaviour and anxiety over her husband's fate, Maya managed to see the night through. Her misery was aggravated by the fact that there was no one with whom she could share her problems. After all, what could she tell any one? Or what advice could she ask?

As dawn finally broke, Maya felt drained of the energy to do anything. Her entire body felt numb and lifeless; her mind was completely blank, unable to think or analyse anything. There is nothing left for me in this world now, she thought.

Vidya went through the morning's household chores and made several unsuccessful attempts to rouse her mother from the bed. But each time, Maya would feign illness and send her off to complete some errands. Unable to stand the antics of the younger one, Maya lost her temper completely and gave him such a sound spanking that Vidya had to rescue him and take him out of the room.

It was hardly nine o'clock that the same clerk arrived again. Maya now had no alternative but to rouse herself. She managed to get herself ready and, taking Basant for company, set off for the court.

She got the mortgage papers attested at the court and returned home. By this time, her psychological state defied description. Her mind was a vortex of confused thoughts and as the minutes ticked by at an agonisingly slow pace, she remained absolutely clueless about the next course of action. The one person who could have helped Maya in clarifying matters was Kedar. But where could Kedar be found? He had been missing since yesterday.

CHAPTER 20

$\mathcal{V}$eena arrived at her new home to get her first experience of married life. The house was filled with the cheerful sounds of laughter and merriment. The entire household was captivated by the bride's beauty. Attending to her needs appeared to be the raison d'etre of all its occupants, from the mother-in-law to the various younger and older sisters-in-law. But their efforts to cheer Veena up, to engage her in conversation met with complete disappointment; not the faintest smile graced her lips, nor did a word escape from her tongue.

The ladies of the house initially thought that this kind of timidity was not entirely unusual in a newly wed girl. Give her a day or two to settle down and she'll be just fine, they thought. But Veena refused to oblige, nor did she show any response to their numerous friendly overtures to break the ice. Veena's complexion, always tinged by a shade of damask, was soon beginning to acquire the pale hue of saffron. The harder the women tried to find ways to cheer her up, the more irritable Veena became with their antics.

Veena's husband was a successful young businessman. And while it is natural for any young man to desire to see his bride on the wedding night, in Brij Lal's case this desire had been honed to a particularly sharp edge. His cousin Channo, who had already described him in great detail to Veena, had also spared no effort in whetting Brij Lal's curiosity by drawing vivid images of Veena's ethereal beauty and warm disposition. He anxiously waited for the moment when he would finally lift her veil and see her charms.

That fateful moment finally arrived. By sheer coincidence, it was Channo – who had prematurely done so much to bring the two souls together – who was also responsible for decorating their bedroom.

The bridegroom entered the room. During the four rounds that they had taken of the sacred flame to consecrate the wedding, and during the subsequent festivities of the marriage, he had only been able to catch a glimpse of her bare hands. His heart had danced at the sight of the crimson glow of henna on the ivory skin. He could scarcely believe his luck that he was now the proud husband of the most beautiful bride in the entire city.

A shiver went down his spine as he lifted the veil to gaze at her. The heavenly flower that his eyes had pined to see was before him – but as a flower that had been separated from its stem, its petals already wilting. It was a picture of the most mind-numbing sorrow he had ever encountered.

Veena had been equally anxious to see this unknown stranger who was now her husband. Channo's daily commentaries about him had only served to heighten her desire for their first meeting. In the temple of her heart, she had conjured ever more elaborate images of her new deity. But her march towards realisation of the fantasies that she had so zealously nurtured since her childhood inexplicably faltered when she was barely a few steps from her destination. Her cherished dreams were mercilessly trampled under the hooves of some invisible creature. She was like her namesake Veena, the musical instrument that sees its strings snap before it has played its first note.

When he lifted her veil, Brij Lal anticipated that she would demur, perhaps act a little coy, and he would be completely captivated by her gestures. But Veena sat completely rigid, her body seemingly devoid of all motion. Brij Lal's friends had coached him fairly intensively on the finer points of handling a bride on the first night. He was, in particular, prepared to encounter a degree of opposition, even an initial rejection of his overtures. But the situation in which he found himself clearly lay outside anything that he had been prepared for. Here was a young man, scion of a wealthy family, who had spent many a colourful evening in gatherings where the popular lexicon made no distinction between the words 'wife' and 'lover'. Marriage, from this perspective, was merely a social licence to satisfy carnal desires! It is difficult to describe the impact of that first look on a person with this makeup, although one can fairly deduce that it must have considerably dampened his initial ardour.

He sat on the side of the bed and gently placed his hand on Veena's shoulder. She remained motionless as before, eyes unblinking as she looked straight ahead.

"Veena!" her husband spoke as he held her arm, still laden with the wedding bangles. "What are you worried about? Come! Look at me!"

Veena stiffened, as though jolted into remembering her present situation. Reacting much like a puppet to his command, she looked up at him.

"I have perhaps disturbed you," her husband saw the apparent unease in her round eyes and said.

"No," Veena replied, as though in a deep slumber.

"You did not like my coming here?"

Veena merely nodded in the affirmative, which could have been interpreted either way.

"Should I leave?" Brij Lal asked again.

"No."

"Should I keep sitting?"

"Yes."

"Aren't you sleepy?"

"No."

"You do know that you are my wife?"

"Yes."

Brij Lal was beginning to lose his patience with the monosyllabic 'yes' and 'no' answers. He could see no sign of the behaviour that he would have expected a newly wed bride to display. He was getting increasingly disillusioned. He wanted to see a bride who would be cheerful, playful, even coy as she said, 'Please leave me…please move away…' etc. But he saw no sign whatever of any of this in Veena.

Not making any effort to hide his disappointment, he got up from the bed saying, "Alright! I am leaving," hoping that Veena would immediately grab his arm and ask him to stay. No such thing happened. As he approached the door, he looked back and inquired, "Shall I leave?"

"No," Veena looked at him and said weakly. Brij Lal felt his male ego under attack. To stay any longer would be an insult to his manliness. He went up to the door and unlocked the bolt. As he pulled at the handle, he realised that it had been bolted from outside.

He turned around, his face by now showing clear signs of anger. Not uttering a word, he saw the hours chime away by on the wall clock, reminding him that this was his wedding night that was ticking away. Still, Brij Lal remained silent. The night eventually passed, its pervasive silence broken only by the hourly chimes of the clock.

At some point during the night, Veena dozed off. It was bright daylight when she awoke, finding herself alone in the room.

She spent three more days and nights in the house. Time appeared to have come to a standstill, and the three days seemed to stretch endlessly into three lifetimes. She learnt on the fourth day that it was time for her to make the customary return visit to her parental home. Far from cheering her up, she found that the thought of going home only added to her gloom.

Veena felt her pulse quicken as she started to approach her hometown. Scenes from her tryst with Kedar two days before her marriage were flashing before her eyes. She found her train of thought take two distinctly separate tracks. One part of her prayed that her eyes would first set sight on Kedar when she entered her home, while another part willed that she should not run into Kedar at all. To clear up her mind, she tried to systematically reconstruct everything Kedar had said that night.

Lost in conflicting emotions, she finally came to the end of her journey as the train pulled into Rawalpindi station. A *tonga* thereafter carried her through the maze of bazaars and alleys towards her home.

During her brief sojourn at her in-laws' place, Veena had initially thought that her sadness would evaporate as soon as she reached 'Pindi, that the gloom would lift and a new energy would flow through her veins. The reality, however, was turning out to be quite different from her expectations. Every step that brought her closer to her home seemed to increase her melancholy. The clip-clop during the journey appeared to come, not from the knocking of the hooves against the tarmac but against her own heart. The anticipated joy of returning home had been replaced by a strange kind of pain that was rending her heart.

As the *tonga* came to a halt in front of her doorway, a certain clarity descended upon her. Before anyone else, she wanted to see Kedar's face as she entered the house.

She met her mother first, clinging to her bosom and sobbing to her heart's content before turning to embrace her siblings. Turning to her mother, she inquired about her father. "Has Bhapaji returned or not?" she asked. But the 'No' that she deciphered in her mother's expression even before she had said a word in reply delivered another blow to her heart.

The other question that came to her lips several times but for some reason remained unspoken was about Kedar, of whom there was no sign in the house. She found herself unable to ask her mother about Kedar despite a burning desire to satisfy her curiosity. When Vidya confided that he had come, and left soon thereafter, she was able to put the query to her mother.

And she was completely taken aback as Maya responded by giving her a detailed account of what had transpired over the last couple of days. 'Have we lost both of them,' she thought.

Maya, meanwhile, found that she now had a fresh source of anxiety. In just four days, Veena's complexion had turned ashen. She wanted to probe Veena about the reason but she was already so burdened with other worries that she felt that she would not have the courage to go into a new area.

Night fell, and lying by her mother's side, Veena abruptly got up and said, "You know, Beyji, we should have opened Bharaji's room to check. Maybe he left a letter or something."

Maya had told Veena about Kedar's decision to go to Kohmari or some other hill station to get a change of climate but Veena doubted if this were the real reason. She could accept that he had decided to leave, but the pretext that he was leaving for a change of climate sounded patently false to her. She had come to know Kedar's nature fairly well and was sure that Kedar simply did not care enough about his health to suddenly take off for the hills. On any number of occasions, she had herself urged Kedar to look after his health and each time, he had given the stock response, 'There's nothing wrong with me.'

Despite Maya's efforts to dissuade her, Veena took the bunch of keys and went off towards Kedar's house, convinced that at least one of the keys belonged to his lock. Maya was attending to her youngest son, who had been irritable and wanted to have some milk. When Veena had been gone for quite some time, Maya tucked the child in his bed and followed her to Kedar's house. She could see that the door was ajar even before she reached there. She figured that Veena must have been able to get in. She was stunned when she entered the room and saw Veena sobbing profusely, a few papers dangling limply in her hands.

Maya ran towards her and stammered, "What...What's the matter, Veeni? Whose letters are these?"

"One is from Bharaji, and the other is Bhapaji's," she wiped her eyes and sobbed.

She proceeded to read out the letters, starting first with the one that Kedar had left for Maya before his departure. It said:

"Respected Beyji,

I was hiding in the stairs and was able to hear the entire conversation that transpired between you and Sardarji. I can fully understand the profound effect that this conversation would have had on you. Surely, you must take me to be a charlatan and a traitor and indeed I have misled you and betrayed your trust. But my conscience knows it, and my God knows it too, that my actions were not the result of any ill intentions.

"I had no desire to unlock these secrets today but now that you have learnt so much through the Sardar, I don't want to add to my sins by keeping you in the dark any longer.

"You see, Sardarji had given me employment at his shop about an hour prior to the arrival of Bhapaji (Mr. Panna Lal) on the day that you had asked him to seek a loan from the Sardar for Veeni's marriage. Believe me, I would have preferred to die of hunger than to accept the offer of employment if I had the slightest inkling of the consequences that were to follow. But unfortunately, I learnt about this only when Bhapaji handed over charge and left the shop, and a little later sent me this letter through someone, which I am enclosing herewith. I felt the ground slip underneath my feet as I read the letter. In a state of shock, I went to the station to search for him and truly tried everything possible to find him. But my efforts yielded no result and I eventually resolved that I could only atone for my sin by taking on myself all responsibilities pertaining to his family. That night, when Veena and Basant came to the shop looking for Bhapaji, I concocted the pretext that he had gone to Bombay. The next day when I came to see you, I again lied to convince you that Sardarji had sent him to Bombay. I left no stone unturned to find Bhapaji, but to no avail.

"When you mentioned that you needed money for Veena's marriage, I went to Abbotabad and sold my house for eight hundred rupees but when I gave you the money, I said that it had come from Sardarji. I did the same with my monthly salary, telling you that this was actually Bhapaji's salary being paid by Sardarji. Other things also went the same way. The fifteen hundred rupees that I paid to your creditor this afternoon was actually to be deposited in the bank on behalf of Sardarji. But I could not bear the thought that this new debt would be hanging over your head like Damocles' sword. Now, there's no reason to be unduly concerned about this matter. I will be able to repay the Sardar's loan fairly soon. I will also send you the remaining one thousand rupees that must be paid to release the mortgage on the house. I am sure that I have the capability to accomplish this.

"I must also confess that when I sought your permission today to leave this town for a change of climate, I was again lying. I don't really need a change of climate, though I do desperately need to alter my psychological state; otherwise, I'm afraid that my life will come to a rather early end. I know that you will be extremely anxious to learn about this strange ailment of mine. But at this stage, I cannot disclose anything more than to say that it is related to the longing for someone and it is to erase those memories that I am leaving this place. I pray that God gives me the strength to overcome this killer longing so that I can once again be around to serve my adopted mother.

"Please do not worry about household expenses etc. I will look after these as long as I remain alive. May God keep all of you safe!

"I did want to see Veeni just once before leaving but......

Yours

Kedar"

After reading out this letter, Veena proceeded to narrate the contents of Panna Lal's letter to her mother.

Like statues, mother and daughter remained frozen in their positions for an eternity. The last few lines from Kedar's letter were resonating inside Veena's head: 'I did want to see Veeni just once....God gives me the strength to overcome this killer longing..."

Veena knew that she alone could understand the true meaning of this 'longing'. Hiding their tears from the eyes of neighbours, mother and daughter quietly returned home.

CHAPTER 21

The waves of a river follow their rhythm of rising and ebbing away and there is no visible impact of its perpetual activity on the water itself. But the banks of the river do get eroded by the waves and seldom return to their original shape. Kedar's life had seen the similar rise and fall of numerous waves, and each had left its scar on the tender banks of his heart. As Kedar set off on this new journey, he hoped that he would be able to heal some of the scars and perhaps restore his mind to its original condition. But did he succeed in this objective?

His longing grew stronger, leaving its scars and eroding the banks of Kedar's life with every step that he took away from Rawalpindi. But possessed with a fairly determined temperament, he did not like to give up easily.

Soon after arriving at Amritsar from 'Pindi, Kedar concluded that his mental state would continue to deteriorate if he allowed himself to remain idle for any length of time. Indeed, a complete immersion in work was the only cure that he saw for his ailment. He reasoned that by doing so, he would at least lose consciousness of his own existence, even if he failed to erase the pain left by Veena's memory. 'What would be the best way to drown myself in the abyss where I remember nothing,' he wondered.

Kedar was also acutely conscious of the heavy burden of responsibilities that he was carrying on his shoulders. 'I must earn as much as I can, as quickly as possible,' he told himself.

He eventually found himself a job at a watchmaker's shop. The manner in which he devoted himself to his new employment defied all description. Despite admonitions from the shop's owner, he would work night and day, oblivious even of the need to eat. Money spent on buying cheap cigarettes and the raw materials for endless cups of tea, and that too without milk, were the only expenditure that he willingly made from his income.

Yet, this was not enough to satisfy him and he felt that he was not saving enough money. Impelled by the need to earn more, he began to show signs of dishonesty by playing around with the accounts. Every now and then, he would even cheat the owner by pocketing a part or even all of the money paid by a customer for repair of a watch. But he was convinced that he was still falling short of his requirements and after six months or so, he quit the watchmaker's employment and started his own little establishment. He had already acquired a considerable reputation for his skill in repairing watches and there was no dearth of customers when he embarked on his own. He would fix even the most dilapidated of watches with such finesse that people would be forced to exclaim, 'Wow! He's truly performed a *kamaal*, a *miracle*! And very soon, that *kamaal* became his nickname, as even the most seasoned of watchmakers started to acknowledge his special talent in repairing watches.

His business grew rapidly, and with that growth, his income also began to rise at a decent rate.

With the passage of time, however, people began to look at him with a degree of suspicion. While virtually everyone in the bazaar thought that he was both greedy and miserly, many also believed that he had some major weakness of character and offered some pretty weighty arguments in defence of this reasoning. Indeed, such thoughts were bound to arise when one looked at this man who earned as much as five or seven rupees daily, yet wore tattered clothes and had never been seen eating a decent meal. His body was so frail that it made a patient suffering from consumption look healthy in comparison. The tea that he drank was without milk, and the cigarettes that he smoked would not have cost more than an *anna* or two for a pack of ten. And on top of this, he worked like there was no tomorrow, refusing to see any difference between night and day.

But Kedar never paid any attention to such criticism. All he wanted was to have his slightly off-key kettle and his pack of cigarettes by his side, caring little about anything else. Lost in his work, he could often be seen humming an old song or two. Or while talking to someone, he would suddenly break into a loud, high-pitched guffaw. His laughter often appeared rather forced and artificial, almost scary, some would say.

There was a room of sorts behind his shop, which served as his humble abode. A small pile of coal sat in a corner of the room. He had, perhaps, never even tried to keep a count of the number of cigarettes that he smoked daily, nor of the number of teacups that he drank. Keeping his shop clean was clearly not a priority for him, and it rarely – if ever – received his attention. Little wonder that every single object in the shop appeared haphazardly arranged, often coated with a thick layer of dust.

Winter had descended, and it had been raining since morning. Kedar had kept both the shop's doors closed to keep out the driving rain and spray. He had a couple of watches that needed urgent attention because he had promised the customer that they would be ready by that evening.

Sitting on his haunches, he was completely pre-occupied with his work. The kettle was within arm's reach, gently simmering away on the smouldering coals. Every little while, he would replenish his earthen mug and return promptly to his work. A smouldering cigarette, tucked between his lips, appeared to be a permanent fixture.

The rain stopped, and a strong sun broke out through the clouds. But Kedar was oblivious of his surroundings. Doors lightly shut, he was immersed in his work.

He had just completed repair of one watch and was now pouring himself another cup of tea before starting work on the next one. As he proceeded to light another cigarette, a beam of sunlight made its way through the crack between the doors and stretched itself like a paved highway right across the length of his room to the wall at the other end.

He was smoking incessantly, and every few moments, he would lift his head up ever so slightly to emit a puff of smoke that would gently drift into the beam of sunlight and take the shape of undulating waves. At times, the waves appeared to have a somewhat circular appearance, and at other times they acquired a more elongated form. But regardless of differences in shape or form, they possessed a singular objective – to ride that paved highway all the way to the doors and escape through the crack into the world beyond. Kedar found his gaze transfixed on the waves. He observed that no sooner had they completed their journey to the doors, a gust of wind would push its way through the crack and send them back along the path that they had travelled. Looking at their uncertain progress, Kedar wondered why the puffs of smoke did not want to stay in the room? Why are they so anxious to escape? And then, he found a reply to his own query. 'Because they will not remain still! Because it is impossible to restrict them behind closed doors.'

Lost in his own thoughts, he was silently humming the lines:

Farewell, O fellow travellers of this caravan
Leave me to my fate now
The lonesomeness of a wanderer
Is part of my destiny

He was still in the middle of the verse when he saw the doors part gently. He thought that it was perhaps the wind that was pushing it open. But the sight of a familiar looking stranger in the door brought both his train of thought and his incomplete song to an abrupt halt.

"Are you Mr. Kedar?" the stranger asked him.

"It is. What can I do for you?" Kedar inquired, thinking that he was perhaps a customer seeking to get his watch repaired. But how does he know my real name, he started to wonder – hardly anyone here knows my name and most just call me 'Kamaal'.

The stranger entered the room without awaiting further invitation and going straight towards Kedar, he bent down to first touch Kedar's feet with his palms and then brought up his hands to respectfully touch his own forehead.

"Excuse me, but I have not recognised you," Kedar said with hesitation, as he looked probingly at this slim, middle-aged man dressed in a simple, clean clothes made of inexpensive, home-spun charpoyton.

"My name is Panna Lal," the visitor said, his moist eyes reflecting a profound mix of affection and gratitude.

"What? You are…?" Kedar stammered as the cigarette slipped out of his hand and fell on the cabinet and unable to speak another word, he went down on his knees and prostrated himself at the older man's feet.

Panna Lal lifted him up and for an eternal moment, clasped him to his chest. Neither man uttered a word, their tearful eyes expressing their emotions more poignantly than mere words.

"Oh my…" Panna Lal started to say more than once as he relaxed his grip on Kedar, only to clutch him in his embrace again.

"You've returned? My gratitude to the Almighty!" Kedar spoke as though in a trance, still unsure if his mind was playing tricks or he was truly seeing Panna Lal.

"But you…" Panna Lal said, using the respectful plural form as he addressed Kedar. "You look so thin…?" he asked as he observed Kedar's gaunt frame and sunken eyes.

"Please don't address me like that, Bhapaji," Kedar said with great humility. "Perhaps you don't know that I am like your…"

"Of course! You are my son – indeed, more than a son, you have been the guardian of our family's honour," Panna Lal interjected to complete Kedar's sentence. "But have you acted like a son, Kedar?"

"So when did you arrive?" Kedar inquired as he evaded the accusation implicit in Panna Lal's words. "Where did you stay? How did you manage? What precisely happened?" Kedar asked in rapid succession as he tried to cover his own anxiety.

"I'll tell you everything," Panna Lal replied through trembling lips, his voice still unsteady. "But first, you must tell me. How have you brought yourself into such a state?"

"This is merely atonement for that sin, Bhapaji."

"What sin?"

"The one that I committed by snatching your livelihood, by pushing you into the jaws of death."

"That was no sin, nor did it need any atonement. But there is another sin that you have certainly committed and for that I am sure you will have to atone," Panna Lal said, his eyes again becoming moist as he spoke.

"And what is that, Bhapaji?" Kedar asked with nervously.

"I will tell you later, but first…"

"But where are you coming from?" Kedar interrupted before he could finish his sentence.

"Right now, I am coming from Pindi."

"And when did you arrive in Pindi?"

"It's been a week or so."

"And where were you all this time?"

"It's a very long story, Kedar, which I will tell you in due course. For the present, just understand that when I left, I had every intention to bring my life to an end but I was unable to die. Partly the attachment to life itself, and partly the love for my little kids stopped me from taking my life, but without allowing me to take a step towards returning to my home. The condition at home seemed to be worse than death itself. Finally, to bring some peace to my tormented soul, I went to Hardwar and decided to spend my remaining years in the service of the religious personalities and saints in that holy city on the banks of the Ganges.

"No doubt, the proximity to so many saintly and spiritual figures did help to a certain extent in quenching the fires that were raging within me but the attachment to home and family pursued me relentlessly wherever I went. I became a fakir and immersed myself in meditation and prayers, performing the toughest of penances without being able to rid myself of the ties to my family. Finally, when even two years of penance failed to free me from the bonds of affection, I set forth for my home. I was afraid that by now, home and hearth would have been reduced to dust, and the children would probably have starved to death. Nevertheless, there was this longing in the heart, if only to see the crumbling walls of my home one last time. So I prepared myself for the worst and decided that I must make the journey, so that I could thereafter bring my life to an end without any regret. But what I saw and heard when I reached home left me absolutely perplexed. How could I know that no sooner had I turned my back on my family that God would usher his own Angel into my home, whose sacrifices would…"

Kedar stopped him from speaking any more and said, "Enough, Bhapaji! Let us bring this chapter to a close. When the offspring does something for its parents, it cannot be termed 'sacrifice'."

"Fine, son. But even the noblest offspring would find it hard to come close to what you have done."

"Please don't embarrass me by speaking like this, Bhapaji. More important, tell me if everything is alright at home?"

"Yes…I guess you could say that everything can be considered alright."

"What is that supposed to mean, Bhapaji?"

"We'll talk about that later. First, you must listen to your Beyji's message."

"Go ahead, please."

"You will have to come with me to Pindi by the first available train, that's her message. Kedar, it really is the limit. You did not even convey your address to her, even though you have often sent her envelopes stuffed with money. What could the poor woman decipher when the envelopes carried nothing more than a post mark of Amritsar?"

"I have deliberately kept my location a secret, Bhapaji." Kedar's heart was pining to know about the welfare of another member of the family about whom Panna Lal had made no reference in his conversation. Several times, Veena's name came to his lips but remained confined within their boundaries.

"But I may not be able to leave just yet, Bhapaji," Kedar sighed.

"Why?" Panna Lal exclaimed at this unexpected response.

"I have not discharged my obligations yet."

"You have not discharged your obligations despite having already sent thirteen hundred rupees instead of one thousand? The house has already been freed from the shackles of the mortgage. You will have to come home with me, Kedar."

"But I still have to pay back four or five hundred rupees from the fifteen hundred owed to Sardarji."

"Sardarji has already waived that amount. And he has taken me back in his employment."

"But apart from that amount, I still owe him some money."

"And what is that?"

"I had acted in bad faith and held back some more money as well."

"Please don't worry about that, son. I know that you did that too for a good cause. I will take responsibility for repaying that amount. Moreover, Sardarji is extremely fond of you. He is very keen to retain your services."

"By once again removing you from the job?"

"No! No! We will both stay with him as his partners. He wants to open a new branch in Peshawar."

Kedar was now in a dilemma. After listening to Panna Lal, he was leaning towards accompanying him to Pindi when he suddenly remembered his reference to another sin and its atonement. "So you were going to tell me that I have committed some other sin too. What was that about, Bhapaji?" he asked.

He saw Panna Lal's face turn pallid as he contemplated a response. A pall of gloom, dark as the evening shadows, cast over his eyes. For a long while, he remained silent. Then, supporting his head with his palms, Panna Lal said, "Kedar! You have done more for us than anyone else on this earth could have even tried. You have saved my life, rescued my family from all manner of difficulties. But, Kedar, you…" The words died in his throat and he began to hiccup.

Kedar's heart was pounding against his chest. Shaking Panna Lal's shoulder, he asked, "Tell me, Bhapaji! What has happened? For God's sake, tell me immediately."

"Kedar!" Panna Lal steeled himself with all the strength that he could muster and said, "You have taken poor Veena's life."

"Veena…Veena…has she died, Bhapaji?" Kedar felt his eyelids drooping and his limbs going numb. When his eyes opened after a while, he saw Panna Lal wiping his own tears. Kedar remained speechless, his eyes once again getting eclipsed by dark shadows.

"What happened to her?" Kedar wanted to ask Panna Lal a thousand times but found himself unable to utter the words. Perhaps, his own conscience was giving him the reply, 'You merciless soul! You are the one who killed her and now you want to know what happened to her?'

Panna Lal started to recount the details without waiting for him to ask. "She breathed her last two weeks before I returned to Pindi. But the words that she uttered in a state of delirium before her death broke your Beyji's heart into bits. Since the day Veeni died, all she keeps repeating is, 'Alas! If only I had known! I would have gladly married Veena to Kedar.'

Kedar did not have the strength to move his tongue. His eyes were open, but he saw nothing. He felt as though his lips, his tongue and his vocal chords had all petrified into one wooden mass.

A deathly silence hung over the shop for a long while, as if there was nothing more to be said or heard.

"None can prevail over destiny, son," Panna Lal finally broke the silence and said. "Come with me and give some solace to your Beyji. She is besides herself with grief."

Kedar remained motionless as a statue.

Panna Lal pleaded again, "Son! I can fully understand your emotional state. You have shown exceptional forbearance. If only once, just once you had mentioned about your feelings for Veeni to your Beyji…" He paused for a moment before continuing, "…or if only Veeni had shared her secret with her mother. But destiny cannot be altered."

Kedar continued to remain paralysed where he was. Neither his lips nor his eyes showed any sign of life.

"Do you know" Panna Lal said, "why Veeni's mother is so desperate to get you home?"

Kedar had begun to recover marginally from the traumatic shocks that he had just received. His pupils moved slightly, as he gave Panna Lal a wane, vaguely inquiring look.

Panna Lal continued, "She wants to marry Vidya to you so that she can truly make you her son. Vidya is fairly mature now. Although a couple of years younger than Veeni, she is taller and looks even older than her."

Kedar heard Panna Lal's proposition and heaved a deep sigh before speaking, "Bhapaji! Veeni has gone! Everything I had has gone! Please don't ever bring up this subject with me, Bhapaji. I….I…" And instead of completing his sentence, he broke into a loud peel of laughter. Panna Lal was watching him intently, recognising that his laughter was little more than an attempt to hide a stack of hay in a raging fire.

"No, Kedar," he said firmly. "You will have to agree, if not with me, then at least with the one you have called 'mother'. I would not expect you to turn down her plea!"

"I will always be ready to do anything for my mother but Bhapaji, perhaps she is unaware that Kedar's soul died quite a while ago. Does she merely want Kedar's corpse for this purpose? That is not feasible, Bhapaji. It's absolutely impossible."

"Kedar!" Panna Lal beseeched him again. "Just come home once. We will do as you say."

"Bhapaji! I will, if I manage to recover from this ordeal," he sighed.

"You will have to come with me."

"Bhapaji, do you want me dead?"

"No, son! I pray for your life."

"In that case, please do not insist that I should accompany you now. My raw wounds will again start bleeding if I go there. I may not even be able to last a day in that place. I want you to understand that, and if you still want me to come, I am ready. Let's go."

Panna Lal heard Kedar's stark testimony in silence, recognising the transparent honesty with which it was delivered and the absolute truth that it carried. Unable to argue any further, he reluctantly gave up his demand.

After spending the night with Kedar, Panna Lal prepared to leave for Rawalpindi the next morning.

CHAPTER 22

*B*efore his departure for Rawalpindi, Panna Lal implored Kedar to take better care of his health. Insisting that his health was more important than anything else, he continued to counsel him on this right until the train gave its final whistle to signal that it was ready to steam off. Kedar responded to his pleas earnestly, assuring that he would indeed pay more attention to his health.

The train was about to leave the platform when Kedar fished a little pouch out of his pocked and slipped it through the train's window to Panna Lal with the request, "Please give this money to Sardarji. I have not been able to work too well this month. My eyesight now does not allow me to concentrate for very long."

Panna Lal opened the pouch to find some currency notes and some small change. He returned the pouch to Kedar and said, "I assure you that he has already waived the remaining amount."

"So give it to Beyji instead," Kedar said forcefully. The argument continued even as the train started to leave the platform, with Kedar managing to prevail eventually by tossing the pouch through the window to Panna Lal as the train gathered speed.

Kedar returned home from the station, bolted the door and went straight to his bed. He did not open the shop, nor did he get up from his bed. Or, perhaps, he was simply unable to get up. He spent the entire day in the grubby sheets, with the stove within arm's reach, and that long suffering companion - his faithful kettle – resting unsteadily upon the smouldering coals. Every half hour or so, he would reach out for the kettle, pour himself a cup of black tea, light another cigarette, and sing the same lines:

Farewell, O fellow travellers of this caravan

Leave me to my fate now

The lonesomeness of a wanderer

Is part of my destiny

He could hear his voice gradually fading, corresponding perhaps with his waning life force.

After lying in this manner for a long time, he abruptly sat up and propped himself against the wall, as though he had suddenly remembered some important, unfinished task. He delved into his pocket but found that it was absolutely empty. He then looked around him, like a drowning man searching for a straw that he could clutch but finding nothing but disillusionment.

He thought of his neighbour, the Sikh owner of a bookshop who would often spend some time with him and who had tried in vain to discretely probe into his complicated past.

Kedar attempted to get up from the bed but his feeble legs failed him. Not finding the strength to go up to the door, he reluctantly returned to sit on the edge of the bed. His chest felt heavy after the brief exertion and he broke into a severe bout of coughing. He was used to seeing a streak of blood in his sputum whenever he coughed like this but today, it seemed that his sputum had been soaked in red. Exhausted by the coughing, he again decided to lie down. He remained in this position as the hours went by and the daylight gradually faded away into dusk.

He heard knocking on the door, followed by someone's voice calling his name. It was his neighbour's voice. Kedar answered that he should release the bolt and come inside but his voice did not have the strength to carry, forcing him to repeat several times before the neighbour eventually heard him.

The door finally opened and his neighbour entered the room.

"I was just thinking of you," he looked at his neighbour and said. "Maybe God does listen to my prayer once in a blue moon!"

Giving his neighbour a beseeching look, Kedar said, "I needed to send a telegram, if it would not be too much of an inconvenience?"

The neighbour quickly jotted down the message and rushed to the post office to dispatch the telegram. The post office was not far, and he added express fee to hasten the message to its destination.

Kedar then proceeded to narrate the story of his life, from beginning to end. His neighbour listened intently, and by the time Kedar completed his narrative, it was well past midnight. The neighbour did not want to leave him alone that night because he could see that Kedar did not have much time left. But Kedar forced him to leave, insisting that his family must be waiting for him. Moreover, he wanted to spend that night in solitude.

As the neighbour left, Kedar poured himself the last few sips of tea from the kettle. Picking up the packet lying near his pillow, he saw that there was just one cigarette remaining.

After finishing the cigarette, he lay motionless for a while. Extending his arm towards the stove, he found that the fire had gone cold and the kettle was empty. His other hand reached for a cigarette but the packet was also empty.

Kedar's breathing quickened, and his chest was moving up and down with his laboured breathing.

He coughed one last time, emitting a stream of blood before his trembling frame came to rest. His body was still now, the head lurching over the side of the bed.

Next morning, Kedar's shop was teeming with neighbours and bystanders. His Sikh neighbour did not allow his body to be taken for cremation until well past noon.

He was perhaps waiting for some of Kedar's relatives to turn up on the train that came from Rawalpindi at half past twelve.

It was close to one o'clock when an elderly couple quickly disembarked from a *tonga*. They pierced through the thickish crowd and embraced the dead man's body. The heart-rending wails of the woman moved even the hardiest bystander to reach for a handkerchief to wipe his tears. It was only with considerable effort that the couple was eventually prised away from the body so that the funeral procession could make its way to the cremation grounds.